Basta

LUCIA MAZ

Published in the United States by La Luce, Los Angeles.

Paperback ISBN: 979-8-9995991-1-7

First Edition.

Cover design by Heidi Richardson

To all the feminists who've paved the road for us;

I promise not to let you down.

April 15th, 2016, Los Angeles, 6:37 a.m.

Nothing inspires change like a swift punch in the face.

"God, Leona," Carlos said as he awoke in terror and rubbed his cheekbone. It was the fourth time she'd hit him in the heat of a nightmare in the last few months and he was worried that the walls were closing in on her. "This has to stop..." he said. "I know you're going through a lot, but I can't be afraid of falling asleep." He groaned and turned over, mumbling, "get some help please. I'll take you."

She shifted and looked at him, realizing what she'd done, and admiring his health. "I'm sorry," she said, pushing one of her dark curls out of her face and falling back onto her pillow. She stared at the popcorn ceiling. It was old and bare in spots. She remembered her dream."I didn't mean to...they were... they were on me again. They never get off."

"I get it," he said, turning over to look at her. He touched her cheek softly. "I am sure it was horrible, but I'm exhausted and you must be too. I can't imagine you're sleeping well with all of this going on."

"I'm not," she said and sat up in a sudden burst of energy. Streams of sweat dripped down her neck as if trying to find their mother lake. "I can't do this anymore." She considered how bruised she was and then pushed the thought as far away as she could."Go back to sleep. I promise I won't touch you."

7:03 a.m.

Lucas didn't feel like a monster. In fact, he was an average guy as far as he was concerned. Women had called him a beast—this is true—but he couldn't imagine they were right. If anything, they were the ones who had become problematic. They used to know when to shut up.

In his boyhood he was fed a steady diet of military dictates, by a dad who had raised them that way. They were good boys who did what they should and followed orders until they were the ones who were giving them. Then, they would take their rightful place as rulers of the earth.

His brothers, Joseph and Tyler, had taken well to the training of their childhood. Wake up at 6 am. Make your bed. Do a 5 mile run. I*'ll make men out of you, if it's the last thing I do.* But Lucas found himself in the shade most days. He wasn't as fastidious and felt that he could never live up to the high and mighty expectations of his father. Because of this he crept into the cave and mulled over his misfortune.

One particular morning stood out to him as the turning point. They had just gotten finished with a run on a festering

August morning when he found himself trailing the pack as usual. Tyler was up ahead and had fallen onto the grass in exhaustion, sweat dripping down his neck, and Joseph was already in the next round of the workout with their dad.

"Of course you're the slowest again. I've been done for about an hour," Tyler said as he saw Lucas approaching. "You're such a pussy."

Lucas forced out a grunt-like laugh and fell onto the grass next to his older brother, his face bright like a punching bag and his long albino limbs stretched out, splotches of rash beginning to form from the heat. Beyond them his younger brother Joseph and The General–that's what they called their father–were doing push-ups to show that the run hadn't whipped their spirits, much less their bodies. *Real men don't feel pain. Real men push themselves.*

"Get your lazy butt off the grass, you worthless pieces of shit." His dad yelled at Lucas and Tyler. Joseph beamed down at them, loving that he wasn't in the spotlight at that moment. Lucas always thought his older brother got the worst of it, being the first and therefore the golden child. Tyler's face formed into a grimace and swung his arm over towards his brother, smacking him in the chest to maintain his place in the order of things. He had been the favorite for as long as anyone could remember. His blond curls bounced as he pounced on Lucas and got up, proving his ascension.

"Yeah, you idiot," he said to Lucas. "The General is talking to you."

The General was a fitting name for their father, a man who wouldn't take 'no' for an answer. He was a machine without a hint of kindness. *Take no prisoners and if someone shows weakness, hit them hard. Never let someone overtake you. You have to be the top dog–there's only room for one.*

. . .

He remembers very little of the rest of that morning. When the family talks about it all they say is that Tyler had it coming and deserved what he got. And all Lucas can remember is that when his little brother hit him he decided it was time to change positions. It was in those minutes–the moments after the violence that landed his brother in the emergency room with three broken ribs, a fractured skull, and a busted nose–that Lucas became a man.

7:05 a.m.

I watched Leona from the window, as I did most mornings. My sweet and lovely granddaughter, Leona, so distressed as usual, like a tiny hatchling fresh out of her shell without a fellow bird to lend its wings. She always seemed so alone. Even in a crowd of people, she was lonely.

She muttered, "Basta" under her breath as she got out of bed.

It was one of the few Spanish words she knew and it found itself on her tongue many mornings as she awoke in terror. I had taught her the word two decades ago when she was just a young twig and she instantly felt as if it held power. I remember her saying it over and over again as if it were candy to be turned by the tongue. She'd scream it whenever someone did something to her that she didn't like and then laugh when they didn't understand her. She was so full of laughter back then.

The word did hold power but she wouldn't know how much until much later in life when her Aunt Cecilia, was murdered in cold blood. We lost my daughter that day in the most wicked of ways, but I had pictures of the heroism she demonstrated before she was raped and then murdered by the man who felt he hadn't already taken enough. After the terror of her death, Leona used to look at the pictures of the protests that people held in honor of Cecilia. They carried signs with the bold word scribbled: Basta. Enough is enough.

Our entire family came up from nothing, so I had to risk it all to make a name for myself as well–we all did.

One of the protest scenes that I showed Leona never left her, as she found herself looking for strength on a daily basis. As we speak she has the picture on her dresser. It sits in a lavish gold frame because that's where it should be. It is royalty.

But this story is about Leona. On this particular morning, I watched her awaken from her nightmare and sit up in terror. As she did so, the sheet she'd been clenching onto fell down around her chest in a heap, and she caressed her neck with her left hand, realizing that strangle marks from her nightmare were nowhere to be found. It was only Carlos in the room with her. As she got out of bed, she seemed to stammer. It didn't surprise me that she was teetering. I think most people would in her situation. They say your body reacts the same whether you're awake or in a dream, so it didn't matter whether the chase was real or simply a figment of her imagination.

Basta
bas·ta 'bä-stä : that's enough : stop it!
Spanish, Italian, French

As she walked out of the bedroom and into the bathroom she looked back to Carlos, feeling horrible about what she had done. Our family's vintage golden key, with the embossed swallow, sat on the dresser where she'd left it the night before next to Cecilia. It was glimmering brightly in the light of the morning, looking quite beautiful if I must say so. I always loved that key. It's Atzi's and what is there not to love about Atzi? I will get to her later on but you should know that she is a queen. We've got a lot of magical women on my side.

I wish I could hold the key again with its intricate edges and the emboldened shape of a swallow in the middle. No one knew what it was supposed to reference, or why the owner had originally placed a bird at the center, but we cherished it as a relic of power and magic. Our family, the Oros, are more into the sky than the concrete, if you know what I mean, and so we chose to give it our own meaning.

After going to the bathroom, Leona snuck back into bed. Carlos had fallen back to sleep and she wanted to be near him. From behind, she quietly hugged him and snuggled in. He was warm and his chestnut hair, all scruffy and loose, sat upon the back of his neck as he snored. She envied his deep sleep. Looking at his neck was some sort of refuge from her nightmare. She had always wanted to be like that–like an old man on a train passed out from the second they chose to. It seemed only men got to have that type of privilege.

Ever since my Leona was young she struggled with the type of anxiety that takes your breath away, but it didn't peak until age fourteen when everything fell into the claws of the behemoth. The monsters swallowed her and spit her back out a raging mess.

You may wonder how I know all this, but all I'll tell you at this point is that we know way more than people imagine us to. We're wise, as they say, so much wiser than we let on. But also, my granddaughter isn't as good at hiding things as she thinks she is, so I guess it was probably obvious to anyone who knew Leona in her younger years.

Carlos had passed out but she did not. She stayed awake, afraid of what would happen if she closed her eyes again. She was afraid of herself. Leona released her grasp and turned her head the other way to peer at the light that landed on her soft blue pillowcase in a thin line, showcasing the tiny songbirds in the design—little imprints of a light and happy life. She inhaled peace. The birds seemingly yearned to fly off the soft material and up into the air. Gazing around the room, she imagined them flitting from one place to another.

Just then, something quickly scuttered under the bed and she caught sight of it. *Probably a cockroach*, she thought. She pondered all that she would have to do that day: class, work, and then more work and the wheels began spinning. Always moving like a tumbling weed in the desert. Nothing to hold onto and blown in a hundred directions with a simple shift of the wind. Outside, heavy trucks groaned down the street, and cars could be heard passing by the flower shops, apartments, street sausage vendors, and empty run-down buildings. No one expected silence on Skid Row. Well, they aren't technically in Skid Row but it is close enough to make that anxiety I was talking about build up inside of her continuously.

As she thought of the chaos outside, the nightmare inside returned to her and she saw it fresh as day.

She had been standing at the bus stop when suddenly the sky turned red and the scenery shifted. Without notice, hundreds of men on horses galloped in dogged motion towards her as she gasped for air and tried to hide, cowering under the shadows created by the moon. There was nowhere to go. The street had turned to a desert, and in it, the vast swath of men thirsted for her. Where were their daughters? Where were their mothers? She thought. In this land, there were no women to be loved or admired, only devoured.

The men rushed after her, lusting for a fresh kill.

Bodies everywhere. Hungry bodies.

We see you. We're onto you, they seemed to say.

Hoping to become invisible, Leona had nestled herself against a dark tree, wanting to somehow become part of it, but instead her body stuck out like the silhouette of a charburned branch.

The blood sky shone behind them as they jumped off their horses and ran like giant wicked spiders towards her, salivating with desire. She heard their footprints messily pounding the sand as if they were giants set to stomp her into dust.

And then Atzi appeared. She was wearing the outfit her grandmother, Xochitl, had described her wearing every time she told the story of the key. It was a long colorful intricately woven poncho-like smock with a swallow shape set into it. To Leona, Atzi looked magical, but the look on her face was one of consternation. She held the family heirloom in her hand and lifted her arm up as if to make a declaration against the blood sky. Seeing this, Leona felt peace fall over her at once, as if a sweet storm had suddenly poured down upon them, but then just as quickly as it materialized, it dissolved along with Atzi. She was nowhere to be found, and Leona found herself quite alone once again in the thick of the desert as the men powered towards her.

Dirt rose into the clouds as her enemies drew nearer and nearer and a ghostlike figure fell from the heavens in a rage of a twirl. He had deeply-sunken eyes and long golden hair that looked like snakes wriggling out to help him in his attempt to devour her.

With a thrust, he reached out to grab her neck as she gasped for air and gagged in response to his grip.. "You want this."

She did not. With this memory, she pulled herself back around Carlos and tried to escape into him. He awoke again and turned to her.

"You okay?" he asked.

"I don't know. Are any of us?"

7:15 a.m.

It took Tyler four months to regain his strength after the attack. This should have bothered Lucas, but it didn't. All he could think of was the fact that he didn't want to slide down to last place again. It was horrible at the muddy bottom. The General came down hard on Lucas after the fight, but he saw a newfound glimmer of respect in his father's eyes–one he shouldn't have held but did, and this acceptance mattered much more than brotherly love. The desire for a father's approval is the love song of many a murder story.

And his older brother Joseph? He was angrier than a tea kettle and secretly vowed to get revenge on Lucas for the harm he'd inflicted on their little brother. Lucas enjoyed his older brother's fury and dodged him the best he could. Joseph had been pounding on Lucas for years and now he seemed to fear him. After this revenge act, he knew the torture would stop. No one would dare. You don't mess with crazy.

At this point, Lucas had it together. He was a grown man and was doing what most people his age did: work all day and relax at night. As he got ready for work on this morning, he considered how much he'd changed and felt a tinge of pride about his accomplishments.

Riverside was hotter than usual this morning, with the rush of summer whispering its promise earlier and earlier each year. The dry cars flew down the dusty highway and hid themselves in brown alleys next to equally earth toned cookie cutter houses. Someone must have thought they would look better that way, all lined up and ginger bread like. The trees were not surviving. No doubt the developer had planned a lush array of green to separate brown from brown but the bone dry trunks were leaf sparse and withering, seeming to bend over to escape the heat. Dust whirled in the air as Lucas made his way past the browned eucalyptus at his front door and over to his beat up pick up truck. It wasn't actually his, but it was his to use while he worked for *Lowers Construction*–that's what the side read–*a division of Great Ways Incorporated.* Lucas popped open the driver's door and slid his way in, lifting his tool belt and his neatly packed Italian sub sandwich over the center divider and placing it on the seat next to him. He'd have to move it later when he picked up Sergio, a worker they'd just hired to finish their new project, but he'd relish in the space until then.

Sweet Home Alabama. That's what kind of day it is, he thought, as he plugged in his phone and scrolled to find the song. He'd only been a foreman for a month and many times it felt like a dream. *Was he smart enough to tell others what to do? Would they ever find out he was under qualified?* These were the questions that spiraled through his head in the late hours before he closed his eyes each night. He usually ignored the insecurity by distracting himself. Last night he watched porn until he'd gotten tired of it and then somehow got into an argument with a single mom who was ranting on and on about toxic masculinity on one of the online channels he spent most of his virtual time on. By the end, he hated her. That wasn't much of an escape but it still felt good to win. He always felt good after putting someone in their place.

The question–*will they find out I'm underqualified*–was one that never left him throughout his days. He had lied about holding the role at his previous job, but luckily no one had called his former employer to check the validity or how long he'd been there. He hoped they never would.

As he moved down the 60 West towards downtown Los Angeles, traffic began to slow. It always did at this hour. There were too many people who worked in the city but couldn't afford to live there or anywhere near the ocean. He was one of them. When he was a teen and the family was still together, he'd lived in LA, but that was before his mom left. When that happened, everything changed. Everything turned down fast. His throat tightened at the thought of his mother. She had been a soft spot in his heart, but now that she was gone, and nothing was left of the empathy he once held.

He could have been good if his gentle boyhood wouldn't have been poisoned, but it was too late now. The sickness had permeated his every vein.

7:24 a.m.

The flower district, where their apartment is in Los Angeles, is known for the unhoused population. There, hundreds of people try to make it through life with their carts, strollers, tents, and all of their belongings stuffed into reusable bags and bundles. Despite politicians' wide-smile promises, nothing ever seemed to change permanently. The city would clean everything up, basically kicking the people out of their draped tarp and flag homes each month, only to see them come back the following week.

I'd been following these thin promises for most of my life, ever since I moved out west from New Mexico. No program ever worked. Most shelters and assistance programs in the city required sobriety, which basically excluded many of the people who lived on the streets. Despite the post-apocalyptic-looking neighborhood, Leona and her family were mostly insulated from it inside her dingy apartment. There had been a few break-ins here and there, which caused her to exist on the edge, but they couldn't move elsewhere. Where would they go?

Miranda, Leona's mother, met her new husband, a sweet and loving Mexican man, Xavier after my son, Gary, left them. Leona was born in Silver Lake, a city in Los Angeles, where we all lived until she was about five. She'd been in San Juan Capistrano for years and had become comfortable with a slower, safer type of life. Years later, when her father left and her mother moved them back up to LA with Xavier, I was personally happy to be near her but I noticed the sadness in Leona's eyes build up when she found herself back in the brambles of the city streets where nothing was secure or stable. Xavier disappeared a little less than a year ago. He was there one day, living like normal and loving his son, Jas, and Leona, and her mother, and then he just didn't come home. No one knew where he was, but they had serious fears because of his undocumented status, and the absence caused Leona's mom, Miranda, to fall into a deep depression, not to mention the sadness it filled in both Jas and Leona's bodies.

I know where he is, but I can't communicate with Leona directly. If I could, believe me I would. It's really tough to know so much and not be able to yell it out. I wish I could scream the facts at the top of my lungs so that they could avoid the deep heart wounds they've been suffering, but it's impossible.

When I *do* scream, it sounds pretty. So pretty that people remark on the beauty. Actually it's quite annoying because no one takes me seriously.

It was getting late and Leona realized she had to get a move on, but it was the last thing she wanted to do. She looked around the room. Because Xavier hadn't ever returned home, and they were still grieving his absence, the bedroom continued to hold a feeling of sadness within its walls. Huge tapestries of 70s bands hung on each of them: Zeppelin, Hendrix, the Beatles, Bob Marley. Xavier loved these bands. Leona looked at them as she sat in silence, contemplating the day. A part of her always wanted to be an artist, but there was no space for it.

Carlos must have sensed that she was awake again because he opened his mouth and sighed, stretching his arm out towards her.

"I guess it's that time," Carlos said as he rolled over and squinted, brushing his dark hair out of his face and smiling a sleepy widemouthed grin. "I feel better...got a bit more sleep. Glad you haven't left yet. Come here." He sat up halfway as the sheet fell down around his waist, exposing his dark chest and drawing Leona in. He leaned over to kiss her with his thick and plump lips. She had the sudden desire to lick them but decided it would be too weird.

"Sorry about hitting you. I want to kill those guys," she said, bringing his attention back to what had happened earlier.

"I thought you were a pacifist," he said, laughing a bit. "You just said that yesterday."

She hit his arm and scoffed. "I am! Well, I want to be, but it's hard when we're surrounded with so much violence," she responded. "Sometimes it seems like the only way to stop it is through more violence."

"That's healthy," he responded, looking intently at her.

She hit him and said, "fuck you."

He laughed and continued, undeterred. "You know you haven't dealt with your stuff, right?" At this, she pricked up against his touch, feeling defensive about what he'd said. To her, dealing with it meant putting it to bed. "Have you thought any more about counseling?" he went on to say. She knew he was right; he'd mentioned this often, but there was no time or money. Plus, it was irritating to hear him scold her. He had no idea what she was dealing with.

She bristled. "When? On my break at McDonald's or when I'm on my way to the office? When should I go? And who is going to pay for it?" she continued.

"Okay, okay, sorry. No time. No money. But still, you've got to do something. It can't be healthy to wake up with a heart attack every morning," he returned, seeming to be irritated with her lack of acknowledgement.

"Well what do you expect me to do?" she asked.

"I don't know, I guess I am wondering if you should fight back. I mean, not necessarily physically because it already happened, but mentally. It seems you need to learn to be more feisty. You know, believe in yourself."

"So much easier said than done, Carlos," she said with a sigh, taking him in while ignoring his argument. He didn't know what it meant to be a woman.

He backed off, sensing her irritation, and turning his face to the light that was streaming through the window. She softened, noticing his discomfort.

"I'm sorry," she said. "I'm just tired."

"It's fine, Ona. I just want you to be okay."

"Well, then kiss me and stop talking," she said. He obliged and leaned in to meet her open lips. She loved his taste and was thankful for the distraction. She dove in. He noticed the shift in tone and responded by tracing her collarbone, effortlessly pulling her to his lips once again. They met tongue on tongue and breathed each other in.

This is where I turned away. After all, their intimate connection is none of my business and it's none of yours either, if I must say so myself. Why are you still looking?

I like Carlos. He seems smart, like a feminist, and Leona deserves that. You'll see. The more you get to know her the more you'll love her. She's unusual, but in the most beautiful way, like that of a distant star. Carlos fits her well because he's wild and philosophical. I think they are what young people call "soul mates."

. . .

Elated and sweaty—this time for good reason—Leona wiped her curly hair out of her face and laid her head to rest on his warm body. He radiated warmth like the smooth side of a black horse standing under a sun kissed tree. He always coated everything with honey, and she loved it like a tree loves its branches, its leaves, its roots.

He felt like roots to her.

* * *

It was time to get ready, so Leona gazed at her tired reflection in the bathroom mirror. The puffy bags under her eyes made it look like tragedy had eaten her youth. Her skin was looser—less vibrant than that of those who lived in Malibu or other places where the rodents didn't huddle at dusk or at least people didn't know they did.

She shook herself out of her daze and applied a generous amount of eyeliner to draw attention away from the sunken purple crescent moons that underlined her eyes. For a moment, she imagined that she was Cleopatra, the queen who had gained the type of independence that was unheard of for women in 50 BC. With this thought, she called down to the porters and beckoned them to bring her royal staff, the one she would use to tell others just what was expected from them on this very day. Her staff was long and gold, bedazzled with diamonds and rubies from tip to finish. She grasped it with elegance and pointed it lightly to one of her servants. *You, please prepare my carriage! I'll be traveling by the river's edge today. Make sure there is enough shade so that I don't become overheated. Thank you for being good to me. And you, fetch me some grapes and while you're at it, have some yourself. You've been quite a lovely companion lately.* The two porters bowed in respect and smiled at the opportunity to accommodate such a powerful and wise, yet kind ruler. She thought all of this and then looked back into the mirror to see an impish woman with black curls staring back at her.

Not quite Cleopatra.

.

I believe I am the closest thing Leona has known to female strength because no one around her has really risen. Not to sound arrogant, for everyone hates a narcissist, and I don't believe myself to be one, but I did really shake things up and roll the dice in my time. In my early days I had been a rebellious trailblazer who didn't take no for an answer. I pushed past all of the cemented obstacles and moved where I wanted to go, always looking for opportunities and never allowing others to steamroll me. *You know they will if they can.*

I moved from New Mexico on my own, with my suitcase and a few boxes, in order to make a better life for my children. I left my "sitting on the cusp of abuse" husband in an exercise of caution, aware that what he poured onto me would soon be dumped onto our children and then maybe *their* kids if I didn't break out. He hadn't hit me yet (should anyone ever have to anticipate this?), but it was obvious which way the wind was blowing. I did what all good mothers hope to do: I ran when I saw the fist in the air. I didn't wait for it to fall on me. My husband had shown signs of pent up anger and lack of self control–such an impulsive and emotional man–but I always wrote it off to the fact that he was a veteran. Then one day as I was leaving for work he grabbed my wrist and scolded me about being late. I'm not sure what gave him the idea that I would put up with that. It caused me to realize that he didn't know who he was dealing with.

The next morning, I waited until he went off to work–kissed him 'goodbye' even–and then I packed the kids onto the bus and made my way to the City of Angels to stay with a long lost friend. Luckily it all worked out in the end. I never heard from him again and we all flew into the bright future, but that doesn't mean it was easy.

I was a singer back then, and I guess I still am today. After years of doing dirty cleaning work at a tiny club in Los Feliz, the owner heard me one night and invited me to perform on the small stage in the early show the next day. It was like a dream. I'd never imagined anything would happen with my raspy voice and the songs of my parents' land. One thing led to another and I soon met an agent who drank martinis there. With this, I got what they call a "big break" and began to see the fruits of my labor multiply. Within a few years of working hard on my vocals and aesthetic I was able to get a record deal that took me on a tour through Mexico. It was a risky yet lovely journey through my parents' beautiful and woeful country. I had to bring the kids with me and I knew that as a single mother with small children, there could be trouble, but I trusted my intuition and made it work. Guadalajara still has my heart. I think I'll go there once things get settled.

Leona wanted to trust herself, but she found it difficult. Maybe when you grow up unsheltered, you can never shake that feeling even once you're housed and stable. Emotional security is another thing. Her dad, Gary, had all types of security with me–at least I think he did–but he didn't pass that version of security on to Leona. He left her and her mother when she was only twelve and she hasn't seen him since. None of us knew where he was. I do now, but that doesn't help much because I can't do anything about his sorry state. It doesn't bring any solace to know where a druggie lays his head, especially if he's your son. It's still full of methamphetamines no matter where it lays.

. . .

As Leona looked in the mirror, she thought of me. She and I have the same black curls and hazel eyes, but as far as Leona is concerned that was the limit to our similarities. I see the layers of us that overlap like a sedimentary composition, but she lacks the confidence to view herself in that golden light. Leona hopes that tenacity was a shared trait of ours as well, but according to her it didn't seem to be. I've always thought that she was too hard on herself, and I am sad that she doesn't realize that I've passed some of my generational energy into her.

I'm sure you've noticed that I am still quite energetic, so much of my energy is still with me. Since my departure Leona has been feeling a tingling inside of her—a hint of strength building up in her core–and she doesn't seem quite sure where it has come from, but I know. It's from all of us. We've passed it down to her, not just me but Atzi and Cecilia, all of us. We're hoping she'll learn how to use it.

Leona is convinced that this growing strength is symbolized by the key I gave her a few years back. Like I said, it has an upward soaring swallow, positioned to move courageously through the sky. My mother gave it to me before I moved to New Mexico and it had been in the family for many generations. It was originally Atzi's (she's my grandmother).

To Leona, the key means vibrancy—the sweet nectar of life, strength in chaos, and calm confidence; in other words, it is everything she hopes to become but doesn't feel like she is.

She called out to me, as she often did in times of trouble. I guess she knew I'd be listening.

. . .

Xochitl,

I don't know where you are but I do know one thing, I love you, and I wish you were here. I remember you said that energy never dies and that makes me think you still might be floating around here somewhere. Are you? I guess it's better to assume you are. Maybe you're a butterfly or or a hummingbird, much like the warrior legend in Aztec culture states. After all, you are a fighter. You were *a fighter anyways.*

I thought of you the other day as I watched a monarch fly by the other day–she spread her wings and flitted atop a hibiscus. You used to love those flowers, I remember.

I'm so tired. I feel like the petal of a poppy, slowly drying up and getting ready to fall off. So many orange petals lying on the ground. Done for.

I know you'd want me to be brave, but I want to be free.

* * *

Carlos walked into the bathroom to brush his teeth and leaned over to kiss her goodbye for the day.

"Don't forget to get breakfast before you leave, sweetie. I know you have such a long day ahead of you and you know how you are when you're hungry," he said.

At this, she glowed in his direction, appreciating his thoughtfulness.

"Thanks, Los," she responded as she pulled him up against her again. "And thanks for the fucking awesome morning. I love having you in my bed," Leona responded. "...makes the day much better."

"Yes, it does," he replied as he stepped back to look at her. "I am sorry for being so insensitive to your nightmares. I care. I hope you know that."

She took him in for a moment, contemplating how to respond. It did bother her that he seemed to brush it off as something she needed to work out with a therapist, but she also appreciated that he was willing to put up with getting hit in the face and waking up with terror as she yelled so many nights. That's a lot to ask for.

"I do know, Love. Thank you for that," she said.

"I think you are really strong, Leona. You're stronger than anyone I know."

"You must know some pretty weak women then," she said and leaned on his chest.

8:22 a.m.

The deeply dark den of the living room was like an open coffin as Leona dreaded walking into it. She knew her mother would most likely be asleep in her ragged chair as usual since she didn't move much anymore. With a mixture of selfish and empathetic motives, she tiptoed in, hoping not to wake the beast. Her mother had all day to catch up on sleep. All she did was sit there and watch cable news–it was toxic for everyone involved. The darkness sucked Miranda into its expanse deeper and deeper by the day, and she became less capable of lifting her head.

As she snuck in, Miranda shifted in her chair with nervous energy, and Leona continued, frozen one second and moving quickly the next like an experienced gray wolf. She grimaced at the thought of waking her mother. Although Leona was frustrated with her inability to move—or do even the basic things in life—her instinct was to protect her like a fish who swallows their young. Nevertheless, she didn't want to talk to her right then. They all knew that once you got Miranda talking, you were in for the long haul.

As luck would have it, her mother's eyes opened with a start, and she stared directly at Leona, mummy-like.

"Where you goin'? You just got home," her mother said in her deep, throaty voice, as the skin on her neck quivered.

"No, Mom, it's morning...that was last night," she answered. Her mother seemed to never know when one day ended and another began. It had become one long and twisted mess like a broken spider web dangling from a patio chair.

"Oh, hmmm...sorry. The days all run together. One lonely one after another. They just drag," her mother said, adjusting her back and stretching her neck out. "You know how that is..." Her neck fat bunched up above her robe where her hair was soppily parted. Leona worried about her mother's weight gain among other things. She had once been healthy and much happier. Leona cringed to think about the rapid decline her mother had experienced since Xavier had disappeared. Sludge moving like mud down a riverbed to sit in the pond.

"Um, not really," Leona responded while moving across the room. She didn't mean to be unkind, but it was getting harder for her to empathize.

Leona turned her back and pulled the curtains open so that the light filtered in, making the mess visible to the both of them. A bomb had gone off in the living room, and no one had cared enough to reconstruct any sense of order. There were stacks of paper everywhere, clothes piled high on the couch, and bags of chips and cookies next to the chair her mother sat in. The floor was covered with everything from hair ties to burrito wrappers. She knew that showing her mother the mess would wind things up, and she felt guilty about that, but she also hoped it would get her moving.

"Leo, shut that," her mother pleaded with a child's whine and closed her eyes.

"Goodbye Mom," Leona yelled, ignoring her plea, and

ducked out of the front door as soon as possible. She knew it was insensitive, but at that moment found it difficult to care.

It is hard for any of us to feel badly about Miranda's state any more. She is always drooping and with her inaction she brings the rest of her family down. Xavier's son, Jas, and Leona really need her to be a leader, or at least responsible to pay the bills, but she was so wrapped up in her own sorrow about Xavier being gone and her life falling apart that she can't muster the strength to be there for others. Instead, everyone else carries her and most of the weight falls on Leona's shoulders.

Miranda hadn't worked for more than a year which made it so that Leona and Jas had to pay for everything. My daughter in law received a bit of money from her disability claim at the grocery store she used to work at, but it wasn't enough to fully house or feed them.

I do have a role in their poverty unfortunately. They would have been able to live in my old place in Silver Lake if I hadn't been such a fool and let my son Gary steal it out from under my nose. Sometimes mothers have too much impossible love for their children. Anyways, the past is the past and what is gone is gone. That house is definitely gone. Whenever I breeze past the old place, my heart aches a little bit and I feel a sadness about what was and what could have been. No point in wallowing though; it doesn't change anything.

* * *

Any dew that found a home earlier had been dried up within minutes of the sun's greeting. It was blazing in its bright blue sky, and as Leona looked down 6th Street, she thought she'd better get moving if she didn't want to arrive looking like she'd just completed a marathon.

It was still early, but the sidewalk was emanating griddle-level heat. She was pretty sure she could fry an egg on it if she had one. Everyone was tired of these long hot days and the denial that humans were the cause of them. So many storms had rushed their way, sliding the temperature from the low 50s to high 90s in the span of a week. Throughout the year, fire upon fire ravished the mountains and valleys from Eureka to San Diego. The erratic weather was one of the reasons she was thinking about getting into environmental law—to help educate people and hopefully save the planet before they were left with a dilapidated Earth, but she had other horrors like inequality and assault echoing in her head. Regardless of the specific injustice she would eventually choose, she knew one thing: she had to make a difference and it seemed like law was the only way to actually make a mark on the system.

All of that was important but today her main concern was getting to school on time and without dizzying herself into immobility. She had been struggling with balance lately as her nervous system seemed to be shutting down whenever it was triggered.

This morning the signs of chaos were everywhere. She noticed there was a used condom lying on the sidewalk next to a torn up shirt near the overflowing trash can. No one ever seemed to empty them and everything stunk, but you could never put your finger on exactly what the origin of the stench was. The filth had gotten worse over the past few years. Poverty was another thing Leona hoped to change. She knew she was idealistic, but she couldn't help it. The little girl who hoped for more and better still lived inside of her, beckoning to be heard. Many nights she'd lain awake thinking about what she should do and hoping the answer would show its face. No one in her family had any idea what life could be like; they were stuck in what life was, and it wasn't good. According to her professors she'd learn about her true path once she transferred to a university and took upper division classes. Leona vowed to listen to the quiet whisper inside of her though—it always beckoned in the silent hours of twilight and it seemed to know what it was talking about. The idea of listening to her inner voice made her think of one of the letters I had written her years before.

After retiring from my singing adventure–it lasted a good twenty years thankfully–I took up residence in Silver Lake and had the sweet little bungalow I mentioned earlier for many years. During these quiet years (before gentrification, mind you) I began reading a series of books and educating myself on the women's movements, both in America and in other parts of the world, and then I began to write letters to my family in order to inspire them. It was the women in my life, especially my close circle of family, that I felt could learn the most from my experiences and the knowledge I'd ascertained throughout my long years of activism. Looking back, I should have written to my son as well. Maybe we wouldn't be in this situation if I had. You see, I had grown up in Mexico during the 70s and we didn't have much of a say at that time. The same was true in America–as I came to understand a few years later when I moved to New Mexico in 1985. What I had thought was an anomaly in my home country was evidently true in many. Women were not seen as full people and most definitely did not have the full rights and freedom that men did. Honestly, men used to run everything and did what they wanted along the way.

One of my letters, the one Leona was thinking about this very morning, was primarily focused on women's intuition. I've never known if we are actually more intuitive than men or if it was just because we've always had to be on alert. After all, if you know you're what's for dinner you're going to hide a lot better from the consumer than if you were the one who was hungry.

One of the things I had written to the girls about was how I had to learn on my own, once I arrived in the States, that only I truly knew what was best for me. I hadn't needed anyone else to point out the direction of my life. In fact, other people's advice was usually something that derailed me. I just needed to listen to myself, pay attention to what I wanted, and then do the thing that beckoned me consistently. So often, as women, we second guess ourselves, but if we truly take the time to quietly sit with thoughts, our decision will come to us and it's not just about deciding; it's about following through and holding fast to that knowledge once we've chosen our path. Men do it all of the time. They make a decision and then plow forward, hell and high water. If things don't work out they pretend that it was all part of the plan. I've learned to develop that type of confidence and that's probably what has gotten me so far.

Each time after I was done writing a letter, I sent these to my girls and then signed it with the stamp of a swallow because it reminded me of the one on the family key. I had no idea how important they'd become to me later on.

The walk down San Pedro Street was long, and Leona thought about how more and more people seemed to be poor while the rich were buying everything up like a Monopoly game, leaving the average person with no way to survive. No one could afford to buy St. James Place or anything at that level because there were already hotel kings sitting there with fat bellies and full pockets.

The smell of urine interrupted her thoughts as it wafted

into her nostrils and she looked up at the dilapidated two-and-three-story apartment buildings on her street beside flower shops, shady drug stores, old pawn shops, a run-down maintenance shop that everyone knew doubled as a hangout for dealers, and a bunch of clothing shops that sold everything from belts to quinceanera dresses. Her apartment was in a two-story building with barred windows and a half-dead grassy area in the back filled with people's discarded chairs and tires. They lived above a flower shop and shared an entrance with an unhoused man who muttered to himself and sometimes to them. He'd been there as long as they had. With endearment, they called him George because he carried a record with a picture of George Michael on it, everywhere he went. He was a true fan.

Hermosillo, a new taco place that had gone up a few months ago, was on her right, and the smell of tortillas wafted up to her on the sidewalk. They sold all kinds of flavor combinations from Sonora, Mexico. The savory aroma made her realize that she had forgotten to eat breakfast and reminded her of Xavier once again. She missed him like fairy tales; no one is able to anticipate how much we will miss the ability to believe in magic without questioning until we no longer do. Xavier was like magic to her because he had everything she had wanted in a dad. He was a great man and an excellent cook. Leona thought of how he had been known for his hot, doughy tortillas and her belly began to growl as she remembered she hadn't eaten. She'd been so focused on escaping her mother's desire to talk that she'd forgotten breakfast. She didn't have any money, so it looked as though she would go hungry until she got to school. There were a few dollars left in her cafeteria account, but that was it.

The aroma quickly turned to filth as she noticed a ragged red rug that was lying on the side of the road. The sight was disturbing as the dirty red rug triggered horrible memories. She suddenly felt ill and rocky.

I stayed back and watched her manage to balance herself. She was obviously faint. This happens to her sometimes and I'm always wondering if she'll be able to make it stop before it takes her. I wonder if she knows she has more control over it than she thinks. I wish I could tell her.

You see as someone who has been through it all and now sees what is important and what is pure nonsense, I can say that I wish more than anything I could direct a fierce river of power into her and give her the strength she needs to see that these memories do not have to sit in her subconscious and throw her into a fit of oblivion. If she only knew how strong she could be, and how to let go of the pain of terror, she might be able to face the past's reflection and walk on by without a flutter.

Dumpster

I don't want to be brave; I want to be free.

* * *

On January 18, 2015 Brock Turner, age 19, sexually assaulted Chanel Miller, age 22, behind a dumpster while she was unconscious on the Stanford University campus.

Miller had been visiting her sister and attended a party with her. She blacked out at some point due to intoxication. At some point, Turner, who was also intoxicated, found her behind a dumpster and brutally attacked her, stripping her naked, and assaulting her using a foreign object.

Two graduate students caught him in the act and detained him until police officers got to the scene. Turner did not admit to attacking Miller and instead hired powerful attorneys to paint the scenario in a way that made it seem like she had consented and also tried to dehumanize her.

After a long court case, the judge sentenced Turner to 6

months in prison. Protests erupted at this verdict and the judge was removed from serving on criminal cases. Miller was never given a formal apology. Her victim statement went viral when she delivered it at the sentencing. She has since become a writer.

8:35 a.m.

In the early years red had been Leona's favorite color, but it had taken on a new role in her psyche ever since the assault. One event can change your association with something, as you know, and that was the case here. As a young girl, Leona had red curtains with colorful ladybugs perched on leaves and a red bedspread adorned with strawberries, but now the color sent thoughts of violence through her.

Upon seeing the rug, her breathing became shallow, and her head began to pound like a drum. Her vision sent her into a dizzying cycle as vultures honed in on her and began to attack her from all angles, coming in for the kill, pulling at her skin, tearing apart her neck, and leaving her breathless. She watched as they pinned her down and tore at her belly until her intestines spilled out onto the sidewalk. Nausea set in, dizzying her until she was barely able to breath. Realizing her state and knowing she had to keep moving, she took a slow deep breath, counted to six, held it for a few seconds, and then released it slower than she had breathed it in. She had to settle her pulse and this was all she knew to do.

She thought back to how Carlos said she needed counseling, but then pushed it away. There was no time for that.

With weak knees, she stood, but the breathing didn't calm her as it usually did, so she forced herself to find the key and trace the swallow's silhouette. This always brought her a flood of energy as she saw the line of her ancestors flowing into her. It was a meditative practice, and I wondered if this is what Atzi had imagined years ago when she passed the key down to my great grandmother. For some reason, I do not think this was her intention–after all, she'd healed without the piece. It was solely a symbol of her innate gift, but I imagined that she would be happy to see Leona using it in this way.

The swallow key was passed down from Atzi, my great abuela, a woman of healing from the old country. In Mexico, they called her a curandera. Have you heard of that? Well, she received it as a gift from a dying man who laid on his bed in shambles suffering from some sort of fiery fever that would not let up for days.

According to family legend, Atzi, came to him as a favor to his elderly wife who had been lying next to him unhinged as she witnessed the moaning for days on end until she could no longer handle it. He'd broken out in blisters because of the damage the illness had done to his immune system. Atzi, walked in wearing her hand woven cloak that displayed a huge swallow on the back and had been crafted out of the local sheep's wool and called to the four origins of the earth. As she did so, birds from around the land began to sing a song of healing and the sun shone down on the man's tiny house in the pueblo.

Within minutes, he cooled and opened his eyes. His display of pain stopped for the first time in ages and he looked at Atzi in amazement. Rising immediately, he went to his chest of drawers and pulled the key off of the candle that it had been draped upon with its long golden chain. In honor of her healing, he bowed and handed it to her saying that it would be better suited to travel with her.

From that moment, Atzi carried it with her, seeing it as proof of her ability to heal and protect those of her village. It became a legend in the town and she was called upon even more as people hoped to see the woman who rescued him from the fiery grasp of death and the key that symbolized the power she walked with. This antique was passed down from generation to the next in the Oro tradition and somehow made its way to me after my parents died. I carried it with me throughout my adventures here and in Mexico as well. I believe it kept us safe or maybe it was Atzi all along. Who knows? It never let me down, or maybe I never let myself down. None of us will know the truth about any of this as truth likes to hide in the ether and refuse to make itself clear. I gave Atzi's key to Leona after our talk about the attack, and I'm so glad I did because it seems to really help her, or at least she seems to think it does. That's all that matters.

The practice of tracing the swallow did its trick this time and Leona was able to continue on her way, ignoring the red rug that had sent her falling into the spiral. She looked across the street and saw a middle-aged unhoused woman with a long dirty pink robe pushing a baby stroller full of what looked like junk but was probably all of her treasures. It brought her mom to mind, and she thought about how close they were to homelessness on a consistent basis.

It seemed her mother would never rise out of her depression and her mother's disability payments were about to run out–that would be the real test. *Would her mother do anything to keep them afloat?* It didn't seem like it. Leona had been contributing everything she could to the family and their rent but it was definitely not enough. Carlos helped too, as much as he could, but he was still helping his own mother and his brothers. Jas did his best, but couldn't work much because of his own depression. Xavier had been helping them so much, but now he was gone, and Leona had to step into the parenting role. To her, it seemed unfair and exhausting to have to parent a parent.

It hadn't always been like this. Miranda was once an ambitious swallowtail butterfly fresh out of the cocoon, flitting around meeting with everyone before she lost hope and fell into hiding. Times had changed, though.

She remembered back to how her mother hadn't been there for her when she needed her the most. "This happens to everyone"—was what she had said when Leona had opened up to her and told her about the rape. Her mom had spouts of putting her daughter first, but it only ever lasted until something else took the front seat. I had watched her put herself first on many occasions, both when she was married to my now absent son Gary and also in her role as a mother.

After Leona's father left to follow his dreams, there had been a sense of predictability in her life for a year or two, but that comfort departed when her mother forced Leona to move to LA so that they could live with Xavier and Jas. Luckily, Leona ended up benefiting from her relationship with them both, but at the time, she was a mess and had no one to turn to.

I should have been there for her in these times. Believe me, I know that now. I was too wrapped up in my own life to notice the extent of her sorrow. Plus, Leona has always had such a strong air about her. Obviously I know a lot of that is just a facade–we all do this–but still I try to respect that display and only go as far as I think the person wants me to. I should have known to push through. She needed me.

We can't kill ourselves over the moves we didn't make, the words we didn't say, or anything of that sort. No one knows exactly what is needed until the curtain falls though. That's when it becomes clear. But of course, then it's too late.

8:41 a.m.

Lucas had just finished high school when his mom left. He'd guessed she thought her work as a mother was done. With Tyler a year under him and thriving as a high football quarterback, it didn't seem she needed to worry about him, and Lucas had made it through school without so much as a scratch from anyone outside the family.

The General, and Joseph–his father's minion–were too much for his mom to handle. Lucas knew this was true for anyone, but especially her, with her punching bag face.

She was a practical woman, and because of this, she was understandably scared of her husband. He was always on her, night and day, making it difficult for her to live with any semblance of normalcy. No one ever said a general would be good at making a home. They were destined for the battlefield and that was it. If there was no war to exist in, they made one for themselves. Family became the enemy. The home a foreign land.

Lucas distinctly remembered one late December evening, right before Christmas–the holiday his mom loved so much–when he had watched The General pound his fist into his tiny mother. She never did anything to fight back. It surprised and bothered him. She was a feisty woman and a fast talker but once the fists went flying she turned into a sponge. He resented that. Women seemed so weak to him, like the quickly evaporating smoke from a chimney. Something like fire shouldn't cave that easily. On that particular night, she cowered in the corner, next to the tree she'd just decorated, and took his father's hit after hits one after another as the ornaments jingled. The reindeer he'd painted in the 2nd grade rang out to him as the bells attached to the deer's neck jingled. Jingle bells.

Why doesn't she fight back? Lucas thought between silent gasps, but then he remembered who was hitting her. No one fought back against The General. He was a force. Just talking to him was a feat that made a person feel like an ant, and his father had the keen ability to smother all dissent, so the consideration of self defense was futile. He watched as his mom fell and hit her head on the coffee table. The realization of this seemed to cool his father's temper as he slowed and moved away from her, satisfied with this work. He wasn't the type who apologized profusely afterwards and begged a woman to stay. He was the type to gloat in his demise.

Lucas always thought he should help his mom, but he never did. He didn't know why and it scared him. What kind of son just watches this type of thing? He sometimes wondered if he was a sociopath, but then he decided she should have tried to defend herself. He didn't enjoy seeing her get beaten, but he didn't want to take her place either. The only person who would sometimes step in was Tyler, but he was usually off with his friends and that was the case on that particular holiday evening. Lucas hated himself for being a bystander but also found himself admiring the power The General seemed to hold over his mom. He didn't want to respect his father, but something in him did. Something he couldn't name. Years later, as he chose to watch porn with women getting strangled, he sometimes thought back to the eerie feeling he had in his chest when watching his dad crush his mom. Was it there all along?

Lucas' attention turned to the road as he approached Boyle Heights. It was up ahead and traffic was easing up. Usually things only got worse once they neared downtown.

"You see that pink mercado?" Sergio asked. "I used to work there when I first got to the city. That place makes the best tamales in town. If we weren't already late I'd say we should go and grab some."

"Good to know," Lucas answered. "Maybe we can stop by on the way back. I'm hoping we can knock this place down and end the day early. As long as we prep everything today we should be all good to go for tomorrow. Hopefully, those lazy assholes got started already."

"You always say to wait for you so probably not," Sergio shot back, annoyed at Lucas' condescending tone towards the workers and inconsistency in leadership. "They're probably afraid you'll go off."

"Well, they should know what to do today. It's obvious I'd want them to start early. Traffic is a beast."

Sergio swallowed the sentence he wanted to say. He knew there was no point in arguing with Lucas. It never ended well and he was happy to have the job. His family depended on it. They needed him to make nice and shut up.

8:48 a.m.

Leona's stomach was growling and she hoped to get to school early enough to grab something. The stop was just up the way, and the street was so empty suddenly that for a moment, she thought she might have been transported to another town. As she waited and basked in the rare quiet, she noticed a sticker of a happy dancing horse on the green electrical box next to the bus stop bench. With a lei and margarita, he looked like he was drunk—or at least in a festive mood. Although this silliness should have made her smile, it caused her nightmare to resurface, and she found her heart racing again. Her anxiety was piping up, but she couldn't quite figure out why. Horses came running at her, their galloping echoing in her ears. A wicked hand was on her throat. She winced.

This is not real. Stay in reality, she told herself as adrenaline pumped through her body once again.

One on one, men were usually fine, but something in the mob hardened them. Men running towards her—such a frightening thought. The fear of being hunted never subsided from her body. Why did it have to be this way? Her stomach growled and she tried to push the idea out of her mind quickly. She didn't have time for this incessant worry. It was ridiculous.

Thinking back to earlier that week, she remembered the man who tried to grab her on the metro. When it happened, she panicked, and instead of moving away in haste, she pretended nothing was going on, and slowly tried to walk in the opposite direction. He followed her as if she were a song bird and he was a consumer of music. It was like he knew she was the type to stay quiet. She didn't want to be that type, but it seemed like her mouth would never open when she willed it to. She was frozen.

There were about ten minutes to spare before the bus would arrive, so she rested her back against a healthy baby tree and tried to relax. It was quite flimsy but she balanced herself against it, careful to not put more pressure than it could hold. She imagined fairies dancing above her in the leaves and soon they came to life and sparkled upon the leaves of the new tree. One of them stopped weaving a turquoise and white blanket on the loom she had carefully perched upon a leaf above Leona's head and peered down at her, sticking her thumb up to signify that she saw her. *We're here with you. You're not alone. We love you*, she seemed to be saying or at least that's what Leona assumed. The sunlight poured through the bustling branches and shadows danced on the ground below.

Oh to be up there and away from all of this, Leona thought.

Just as she was beginning to feel rested her phone buzzed, and she looked down to see what would probably be the first of many voice messages from her mom. It was a normal part of her day to hear from her via text. It was also one of the most annoying parts.

Hi Sweetie, I just want you to know that I didn't like how you said that Jas has been struggling since Xavier left. He didn't leave, Leona. He's just gone. ICE probably took him. You know that. We have to believe he's out there somewhere. Xavier would never just leave us—not him. He's not like that. I know we were fighting the morning before he left but I still think he'll come back. You should too. You have to have faith.

Leona paused in irritation and then continued reading. Her mom was responding to something she'd said the day before. She never let anything die. No topic was too small to mull over. All her mother had was time and she used it to overthink.

I do feel so bad about our fight that morning though. I wish I wouldn't have said those things. You don't know how mad I was, Leo. I said that I blamed him for leaving our comfortable house in San Juan. I said that he was a failure. I said so many things. I wish I could take it back. I hope he didn't leave us because of that. Or maybe it's the reason he hasn't returned. I just can't forgive myself.

*And Jas...he used to be so happy. I blame myself for that too. He was a happy young man before he lost his dad. I should have gotten a job. I'm such an idiot, Leo. I should have tried harder. Xavier was working so hard, and I was just....*she stammered on as she broke into tears. *I just blamed him.*

Leona felt bad for her mom and hated to hear her sadness but the whole thing was exhausting. It was true, what she said: the night after the fight between them. Xavier never came home. At first, they all wondered if he'd left because of it, but no one could believe he'd do that. After a few months of wondering where he was, they learned that ICE had shown up at his job and had done a sweep. They had to assume he was in it, because he was undocumented. From what they'd gathered, it seemed that ICE always allowed a call, and no one had contacted them, so there was no proof he'd been taken. Even after reaching out to Xavier's family in Mexico and asking everyone who knew him, they came up with nothing. No one had heard a thing. The mystery sat fresh on their doorstep, ripe with anguish, and Miranda blamed herself completely.

She texted her mom with a scowl on her face and some pity in her heart: *Sorry you're so sad, Mom. Don't worry. Things will get better. I know they will.*

She didn't know if things would get better, but it was the best consolation she could muster.

A work reminder popped up on Leona's phone. She had set the reminder on her calendar the day before: "Don't forget to get candles for Garcia's birthday celebration today."

Oh yeah, I need to remember to grab them, she thought. *But why are they asking me? Everyone else has a car,* she continued in irritation. She was an assistant, not the office manager. She made a mental note to grab candles after class. Maybe she could find a party shop somewhere on the way. Just one more thing to do.

As she retreated into the leaves above her again, she saw the crisp blue sky looking back at her and had a glimmer of hope for a moment. The sky was always there, beaming at her with a fresh face as she ran through her wild, unsettling days. A naturally-formed umbrella of leaves shielded her parched skin. The Earth was wild with humans, but the sky was peaceful. She loved that peace. *So much blue. So much space,* she thought. There weren't many trees around, so she deemed herself lucky to have found one and sunk into it. The tree provided a minimal amount of shade because of its youth, but regardless, it felt good against her back, and the leaves sheltered her from the blazing hot sun.

Above, a flock of crows flitted aggressively in the open sky, cawing loudly—the kings of L.A.—as a particular elderly tree across the street caught her eye—an old father oak. It towered up to the 4th floor of the art deco style building next to it, stretching its chest proudly as its branches reached up to the sky, leaves hanging towards the earth with green fingers glistening in the sunlight. She knew it had lived thousands of days and heard thousands of voices below it. *How many of those voices were like hers?* she thought. She imagined an entire forest multiplying in front of her eyes and swallowing all of the pain of the city, covering it with shelter.

Leona was in her fourth long year at L.A. City College, and by all standards, she was behind. Regardless, I was proud of her because no one else, including myself, had ever stepped foot in a college class. Hell, we didn't even know how to enroll. I remember when Leo said she wanted to go, I was surprised and a little scared for her. I have always loved learning and I've read so much, especially about feminism and the women who push us forward, but I never thought any of us would go to school. I guess Leona had wilder dreams than me. I love her for that.

Currently, she is about halfway done with her undergraduate degree. She'd started at a community college because it was the only way she knew to get in. She planned to transfer to somewhere that would set her on the path to blossom like a fat squash, sprawling out with thick and spiky branches. When she told me she wanted to go to school, UCLA was one she dreamed of. I think it's because I took her to the book fair there a few years earlier. She always loved reading.

"What are you doing here? This is my place..." a disheveled man asked, interrupting Leona's day dream.

He was dressed in someone's thrown away t-shirt and jeans, and he smelled like the alley. She looked at his eyes–something everyone who lives in a city knows you're not supposed to do–and envisioned the men on horses again rushing to grab her throat. She gulped. The smell of alcohol and urine hung in the air like a curse as she tried to duck out of his way. He haunted her. She looked away, pretending that she didn't hear him, and tried to remain calm. *Should I move? Should I stay?* She thought, stuck in inaction once again.

"That's mine," he prodded, and began to try to nestle himself up against her or the tree; It didn't seem to matter which. "What are..." His words trailed off. He looked to have forgotten what he was going to ask but she wasn't curious to find out. She thought about how to move away without seeming afraid because her fear might prompt him to get more aggressive. The animal awakens when fear is present. Holding her bag close against her, and using it as a shield, she stood her ground. His eyes bored into her as he leaned in and reached his zombie hand out.

Men on horseback. Fire red skies.

Her world began to spin, and she lifted a leg to move but as she did, he plopped himself down on the ground next to where she was standing. With this shift, he began talking in a nonsensical manner. For a moment, she breathed a sense of relief. *Maybe he'll leave me alone,* she thought.

"CVS is across the street. I go there sometimes. My woman, she's out there," he stammered. "It's warm. You made it warm. You know, I used to have a woman," he said, oblivious to her discomfort. "I'm just happy to be here. Home is where the heart is. That's what my mama used to say. Do you have a home?" he continued.

Without notice he swung his arm up and tried to reach hers.

Basta, she thought.

This action brought images of her aunt's assault to her mind. She fell back into the world of pictures where her aunt's followers were protesting. The golden frame that sat on her dresser and held this moment, flashed before her eyes. In the picture her supporters had been marching and yelling "basta" at the top of their lungs. *No more harassment. No more femicide. No more rape. No more violence.*

He's not going to rape me. He's just an unhoused man, probably innocent, she thought as she tried to steady herself and focus on being strong, not reacting. *Why do I always think the worst?*

The Fearless One

I don't want to be brave; I want to be free.

* * *

Nirbhaya, a 23 year old physiotherapy student, unknowingly boarded an off-duty bus in Delhi with a male friend in December of 2012 after watching a film at a nearby mall. The six men on the bus proceeded to take turns raping and beating her as the bus made it's way through town.

After raping Nirbhaya, they assaulted her with an iron rod and caused internal bleeding. Her male friend was also badly beaten. The two were dumped on the side of the road and left to die. She died a few days later from her injuries. Her male counterpart survived.

When news of this brutal attack got out, many young Indians took to the streets and protested which eventually led to new stricter anti-rape laws. Of the six perpetrators, one of them committed suicide in prison, one was released after serving three years in juvenile court (he was 17 at the time of the attack) and the other four were hanged in 2020.

All around the world, people heard the news in dismay and discussed the horrible details of the assault. Unfortunately, it wasn't the first time something like this had happened and it won't be the last.

8:55 a.m.

All Leona ever thought about was escape. This loop of anxiety and dread, mixed with hope and aspiration, fueled her constant motion and desire to climb, but when disaster struck she often found herself stuck in place.

In this moment, with the man reaching out to her, the unyielding knot in her stomach made her wish she had wings so that she could fly up and out of the mess of the city. She managed to wiggle her shoulders as she thought about this, and it worked, as the long feathered wings that had bunched together behind her back opened up and she rose deeply into the sky, looking down on those who remained on the shattered and withering earth beneath her. She waved goodbye and noticed the light feeling that filled her chest.

A few onlookers glanced at her, and for a moment she thought she was actually out of the man's reach, but then she realized he was still reaching out to her with a look of confusion on his face. Then she realized the bystanders weren't looking at her wings, they were watching him try to touch her. Her feet were planted firmly on the ground where they'd been all along. She looked at the people around her and wondered if they would do anything to help if things got dangerous, but then she remembered where she was and who she was, and that no one cared. They never seemed to. Just as she anticipated, their eyes left hers and focused back on their phones within minutes as his hand continued to grab hers. Her heart thumped and twisted, pretzel-like, as adrenaline pumped through her veins and her feet became ice blocks.

I need to run, not freeze, she thought. She pulled herself out of his reach and somehow got her legs moving.

"What? Where are you...Samantha, I need you," the man pleaded childlike as she began to walk. He stretched his arm out to try to hold onto her, but she had already gotten some distance and pulled away without much effort. "I was going to say sorry..."

The terror kicked in and the men on horseback came back.

Just move. Go. Go. Go, she thought.

It felt like he was still touching her. *They* were always touching her. Slow foot stomps echoed in her memory—the steps of what seemed to be giants pounding through the streets behind her as her brain shrunk deeper and deeper into the expanse of her skull.

Her vision faded, and she became an empty vessel, a hollow shadow of herself. With this dizzying thought, she broke into a sprint.

8:57 a.m.

Lucas' mother wasn't the only violence he'd been a part of. There was also Madison.

When he first laid eyes on the slinky blonde there seemed to be something special in the air, a feeling of familiarity that he didn't recognize as submissive until much later when he saw her lying on their kitchen floor bloodied up and desperate, much like his mother had been when he was a child. He had thought it was the sex appeal that drew him. When they met she had a way about her, moving along the perimeter of the pool table, stick in hand and ready to shoot what could possibly be the best shot of the night. He took her love of the game as a sign of social prowess and decided to join her, curious about what lay beneath the surface.

When he first approached she gave him the cold shoulder. He liked this, more to work for.

Can I join you? Looks like you're on a roll. You have beautiful eyes. It was something like that. He couldn't quite remember. After a few minutes when each had taken their turn, she looked up at him and smiled. All he remembered was that smile, one that seemed to say "come in." He loved that look. Sometimes women gave him that kind of attention, but it was rare. He wasn't much to look at, with his blond shaggy hair and blotchy red skin. He was thin too. Women didn't have much affinity for his slight figure.

In the beginning, Madison made him feel like a man. She seemed to puff him up and it felt good. There was something about her, an innocence as if she wasn't really an adult, although she was well past thirty, that drew him. Her googling eyes, her soft touches, her reliance on his compliments and safekeeping, that made him feel stronger. She didn't seem to know how to do anything on her own. She couldn't pay her bills on time, didn't know how to drive properly, had no knowledge of the world or politics, and seemed to kiss the ground he walked on. She told him that he was her big strong defender. And he was too, until he became the person she needed protection from. The same doggedness he showed in protecting her from other men and the world around her was turned on her when she disagreed with him. He hadn't known he'd react to her dissent this way–it just boiled out of him before he could stop himself.

She kept coming back to the trough of abuse even after he'd shown her who he truly was. That was her fault. He didn't have her on a leash. In fact, many times she seemed to deserve it. She was much less intelligent than she initially gave the impression of being.

In the beginning he loved her, but years later, she simply reminded him of his mother. Another weak woman.

Something about her crumpled skirt between her legs and her cowered head did it for him. In this, he felt a sense of strength burrowing into his chest and he found himself able to feel strong, much like his father had.

Sometimes he wondered where Madison was, but mostly he just didn't care. Women were a dime a dozen.

8:59 a.m.

The world continued to take on an ethereal hue as Leona pounded through the streets. She'd gotten herself so wrapped up with anxiety that she no longer knew where she was, and the unhoused man's hand still felt hot on her skin.

He deserved to be punched, she thought.

Carlos' words from that morning flew back to her. "I thought you were a pacifist?" *Why was violence always on the tip of her tongue? Was she truly a pacifist?*

The large arches of a McDonald's came into view up ahead, and her breathing began to slow as a response to seeing something familiar. She had worked at the company for years, so it was a second home to her. The fact that a fast food joint calmed her psyche was a little disturbing, but it worked.

As she got her bearings and began to breathe freely again, she paused to search her phone for the next bus stop. It was on Hope Street just a few blocks away. She would probably be late to class, but realized that if she ran down the alley, turned right, sped around the block, and got over to the other stop without hesitation, she might make it. She bolted. Something loosened as she did so and hunger surfaced in her. Her body felt as if she was a silhouette and a large body of water had opened up inside of her, swallowing the person she once had been. She didn't know how to act differently—how to respond with strength. With her heavy bag banging against her leg, she continued to rage forward although it didn't feel as if anything would ever get better.

It was hard to watch Leona in this moment, and I say this with the most love possible. She looked hopeless. *How did we create this panic in her?* I thought. *How did we leave her this way?*

I guess it was mostly her mother's fault, or for that matter, my son's, but I felt like we all played a role. None of us taught her how to deal with fear. None of us took her by the hand and showed her the way. It's true that things were stacked against her but it's that way for most of us. Don't you think?

Leona turned the corner and let out a gasp as the bus she needed to take pulled away from the curb. With a powerful burst of energy, she sprinted, waving her hands in the air as she tried to get the driver's attention, but it was too late. It moved ahead, spewing exhaust into her tired face. She fell to her knees.

Xochitl,

I can't do this anymore. There's too much. You know, just too much struggle. And I'm supposed to be the strong one. Who ever said that? Why do they think I'm strong? I'm just a kid. I know I'm old and supposed to be all wise and shit but I'm not.

I already dealt with the terror of a nightmare earlier this morning. There were so many of them. There are always so many of them. Carlos says I need to go to counseling. I'm sure you would agree, but I can't. I just can't make myself do it. I don't like how he doesn't understand that it's not that easy. Maybe I don't want to unfold the past.

Why can't I be like Cecilia, or like you! When that idiot reached out to me, I was ice instead of a raging river. I'm so weak. My chest was frozen, almost making it impossible to breathe and my head was spinning as if on the kid's teacup ride. I feel helpless, like I can't get them off of me. Why can't I be strong? Please help me. Give me strength. I did get away, but barely. Who knows whether he would have attacked or not. Who knows what his intentions were. He yelled someone's name so he was probably just high on something and thought I was someone else, but still I should have done something. I'm so sick of this.

I wish I was a bird. I want to be that one you loved so much, the kestrel. She was so small but so fierce. Such a beautiful little wise bird.

Of course, this reminded me of a letter I wrote to Leona about Gloria Steinem and her propensity to compare humans to birds with two wings. She explained that we were able to fly if we had two wings, but half of the population–women–only had one wing to utilize and that's why things are so much harder for us. We are not equally capable, but it's not because of physical or intellectual inability, but rather because we're held down by a variety of inequities and discriminatory systems, not to mention the very real and common sexual assault many of us deal with in our lifetimes. We're seen as weaker and less competent no matter how much we prove these judgments to be untrue. Our access to equal pay, safety in merely walking down a street, ability to afford child care so that we can support ourselves, and networking capabilities in the workplace are limited by an entire host of unwritten rules that we're born into and that most people ignore.

But don't let me get off on a tangent, the bird Leona is referring to–the female kestrel–is a special one to me in that she is tiny, strong, intelligent, and so much more competent than what we make her out to be. I've seen her fight off a barn owl who was twice her size and outperform her mate in finding food and shelter for her babies. She is exactly the bird Leona needs at this moment but they're not as common as you may think, although many of them live in California. They're native to this land but as you know, or should by now, there are no forests in the city, and therefore very few trees for one to nest in.

* * *

Leona felt something new flow into her; it moved from her head to her legs, and with it she flew quicker than before, like a locust rather than a grasshopper. Her wings were starting to push through her sinewy flesh and her heart burst. She grasped Atzi's key in her pocket and felt it aglow with magic. In this, a door opened.

I'm sure you're wondering how this beautiful young woman got to the spot she's in and why her teeth chatter at the smallest hint of chaos. I wish I could calm her, but I have no power. The story is complicated as I'm sure most of yours are. Humans are not hotcakes.

Part of her story is my story because some of this involves some level of epigenetics. At least to some degree, we are who our ancestors are, and we go through what they've suffered regardless of what transpires in our lifetime. We flounder on the same shores as our great grandparents did but don't know why. Maybe we stutter or have an affinity for the soft breeze of coconut, but don't know the origin of this. Much of it, in my opinion, is due to the carefully woven strings of DNA we all find within our bodies.

Sometimes the terror our relatives have faced follows us into our newborn bodies and just keeps on suffering there. It's as if Dante's inferno never stops burning. This is a new type of purgatory.

And our family has been plagued with sexual assault. What is older or more common than that?

For the billions of women who have walked this fire-dry earth, from the highest peaks to the lowest ravines, from the beginning of our time as homosapiens, there has been force on the female body. A physical, unwanted, force. The legs have been shoved open and foreign objects have been thrust into us against our will. The screams have been ignored and the pain swallowed.

So when you wonder what is wrong with Leona, there it is.

It's not just her suffering, it's all of ours.

It was mine and my daughters.

It may be yours too.

I sure hope not though.

But the chances are, it is.

Las Hijas de Violencia

I don't want to be brave; I want to be free.

* * *

Sexual harassment is so prevalent in Mexico City that Las Hijas de Violencia (the Daughters of Violence) have taken to confronting the men who harass them with confetti guns and punk rock. When a man catcalls them on the street, treating women as objects and trying to justify his behavior, they respond by calling it out and explaining that they feel violated. They express that they aren't okay with men speaking to them as if they are about to rape them. They sing a Sexista punk song and look their tormentor straight in the eyes as they do it. This is purposefully done in broad daylight and in crowded places to hopefully encourage the men to feel ashamed. The men are usually quite shocked as they are used to getting away with it and therefore don't expect the confrontation.

The Hijas de Violencia aim to use comedy in the confrontation in order to take the power back and avoid feeling violated for the rest of the day. If the men can't upset them, they know they've won a little and it moves them forward. With this, they are bringing awareness to the staggering statistics of rape and harassment in their city. In 2017, the UN Global Women's forum ranked Mexico the 6th worst megacity in the world when it comes to harassment and assault. In 2022, Reuters found that 70% of women over the age of 15 experience some type of violence in Mexico.

9:11 a.m.

Leona knew the metro was her last bet in getting to class on time. She moved towards it as fast as her dragging legs would carry her, feet pounding on the hot and dry sidewalk. Time was ticking by, melting into oblivion and so was her chance of getting to school on time. Luckily, the train was waiting for her when she got to the platform. She boarded loudly and crashed into a seat, out of breath. Class started at 9:30 a.m., so she would have to speed through everyone and get there as fast as she could. She mapped out the walk in her mind: get off of the metro, book it down Vermont, rush upstairs to the cafeteria to feed her belly, and then rush into class as fast as possible. She couldn't be late again, that was for sure. It wouldn't be her first offense. Her lack of punctuality was a festering wound in her life.

A charcoal-haired middle-aged woman with a face full of freckles glanced over at Leona and nodded in her direction as their eyes met.

"Woo, made it," Leona said to her. "Crazy day out there."

"Yeah, *every* day is crazy," the woman said in agreement and sighed before turning to gaze at the bustling city streets once again. Leona noticed the woman had grocery bags with Doritos and lettuce sitting next to her heavily-worn blocky black restaurant shoes, and she thought about how she probably had a whole family to feed. So many people in the city worked the graveyard shift, maybe she was one of them. Looking at this woman was like looking at herself thirty years in the future. She shuddered at the thought as poverty and exhaustion weighed down on her. There was a sudden sense of urgency.

Will I ever get out? She thought.

And with this thought she looked outside and saw a hundred women marching in rags in an ant farm-like line trying to get to food, trying to feed their hundreds of children, trying to sleep through the night, just trying to breathe. *How did it get like this?* She thought. *How did we become so unimportant? We're half of the population, seems like we should have more power.* She could see the women's hunched backs and weather torn faces, and she also noticed that their eyes fell to the ground as men in uniform handed out their bags of uncooked rice. There were no vegetables to be found. A fight broke out as one of the bags tore open and some rice poured out on the asphalt. One woman blamed another for tearing her bag and people began to shove one another. The nightmare could not be her future. She vowed to get out. She would not spend her days standing in someone else's line.

* * *

A fly cannot understand how it feels to be stuck in a web until it can no longer move its wings. Do you see this? I'm sure you've been in this situation before. We all have. Our struggles vary but the act of struggling does not. This is how Leona felt; she was frozen in her struggle and she knew it.

I envision that she can rise and become a woman of power

and purpose, but she doesn't see the way. You can repeat something a thousand times to yourself, but if you don't believe it, it will never take hold. She needs to get to a spot where she believes the story she is telling herself.

Leona's stomach twisted in anxiety as she sat on the metro and thought of everything she didn't have. As she considered this, food moved to prime position. She was starving.

A community garden caught her eye out the window. It seemed to be flourishing and the thought of eating vegetables brightened her spirits for a moment. She thought about a garden her class used to tend to in San Juan when she was younger. One of the coolest things they grew were artichokes, which she hadn't seen before the day her teacher showed them to her. No one in our family ate anything as exquisite as artichokes. Those were for the rich. Although I had a good sum of money saved up after my tour when I was living in Silver Lake we still never ate those things. I think the environment you grow up in dictates what you put in your belly.

Darkness filled the compartment of the metro as it fell underground. The light came in flickers. To Leona, it always looked like it wanted to reach out, like a slowly rising sun, but as she stretched her arm to pull it closer, it seemed to shrink into the distance.

The dim light of the cabin made her think of Jas. Lately he had been on her mind a lot as he was struggling with his depression more than usual. Before Xavier's absence, he got caught up in the streets for a short time—probably as a way to feel connected to other people after his mom had taken off with her boyfriend—but when his friend was shot by a rival gang member, Jas crumbled. He watched him die, slowly bleeding out like a river post-storm with his heart pounding ferociously and his eyes leaking as he stood there with no way to save him. What can you do with a bullet wound to the chest? There's no tourniquet that will heal that bloody hole. There's nothing you can wrap around the sorrow.

By the time the cops got there, the perpetrator was gone, and they were questioning everyone around, including Jas. He couldn't take it. He sank into the sand beneath his feet. He didn't speak for a long time. When he did make a sound, his voice cracked from lack of use, and the words came out mumbled, half-spoken. The bright and happy person he was before survived only in slivers. Her mom was right about that. When Xavier disappeared, Jas fell right back into the darkness he'd experienced as a child. Although he tried his best, he was always fighting to get out of bed.

The metro moved up and out of the darkness and colors flooded Leona's view. She noticed the buildings were like markers for different stages of life—vibrant, exhausted, forgettable, new, and tattered. There was an unhoused encampment up ahead. It seemed to change daily in looks but not quality. Today it had a huge real estate banner wrapped around one part of it. Leona imagined it wasn't what Jenny Rodriguez from First Team had envisioned when she purchased the banner.

Suddenly, the sound of a man's voice infiltrated Leona's headspace, and she was shaken out of her contemplation. The man's hand from the bus stop reached to grab her as two brisk talking men hustled onto the metro, the sound of their voices rocked her back into a state of fear.

Basta, she thought.

Instinctively, she moved away from them, getting up and choosing a seat further down the car. Surprisingly her legs worked. She needed comfort, so she found the key and traced the glimmering gold swallow with her fingertips, touching the sharp end. *If I need this, it could come in handy*, she thought as she looked at the men and then brushed the thought away just as quickly as it had come to her. *Violence is never the answer*, she told herself.

At that moment, my words came flooding back to her, and she remembered our conversation after the assault.

'Your bravery will bring you freedom.' I had said this, and I believed it at the time, but I never knew she'd think about it over and over again, or that it would ring in her mind whenever she felt weak. I was happy I had helped. She'd recently reframed it in her mind, however, saying that she didn't want to be brave, but rather wanted to be free. I liked this as a sentiment, but it's also true that as you put yourself out there you see how strong you are.

Of course, none of us should have to be brave. She's right about that.

When she first told me about the assault, I was so upset. I couldn't believe that she, like so many other women I love, had experienced violence to her body and soul. Her attack was way worse than many others though because it involved more than one wicked man. Her trauma was crushing. She didn't even have time to blossom into a flower before they stamped her out like a weed.

"They messed with the wrong girl," I had said as I wrapped my arms around her. "You're not going to let this get you. Do what you need to do. Your bravery will bring you freedom. Don't give in. Mourn. Scream. Get it out. Get angry. Hit something. Write about it. Talk about it. I'm here for you. Whatever you do, don't keep the terror inside of you. I believe in you. You'll get through the fire and come out stronger.

Please fight back. You have to. It's the only way." It was at this moment that I handed her the key. I had been meaning to give it to her for some time but hadn't found the right moment.

I already knew I was ill at the time, but hadn't told anyone yet. *Why bother your loved ones with bad news earlier than they need it.* They said I had a few more years in me and I believed them, so I kept the little secret to myself. Leona needed the heirloom much more than I did anyway, and I knew Atzi would have approved. She had come to me in a dream and made herself clear. This is what had prompted Leona and my conversation in the first place. After waking from a dream, I went to Leona and asked if she had something to tell me. She did.

Our family practice had been to give the key to a younger female relative in a time of need and then continue to do so generation after generation so that the energy could be passed down and would hopefully help them in the moment of need. Believing in the power made it all the more real to us. When Cecilia was raped I gave it to her and she used it to help her heal. It did her well, just so you know. She died but it wasn't until she'd made a substantial mark on this planet and had influenced a lot of people. When she died, we all mourned. *Why did it have to be this way?* On her death bed the key sat in her palm and I believe some of her strength flowed into it. I felt this glow for years after her passing. That's why when Leona told me about her attack I knew what to do. After all, the women in this family are strong but we haven't done it on our own. There's some magic involved.

With the past in mind, Leona held the golden key between her fingertips and looked at the men on the bus. She placed her thumb on the bird in the center as her heart beat hurriedly. The men were completely oblivious to her observation of course because they had done nothing wrong besides having an accent that sat poorly in her mind.

She meditated on its past as tears fell against her will, and then she brushed them away and steeled herself.

Sometimes time doesn't heal; sometimes it cements.

The metro stopped and the men stepped off, oblivious.

9:25 a.m.

When they pulled up it was 9:25 am–way too late for a construction start. Luckily, Lucas's supervisor wasn't there yet. He'd have to get the guys working quickly to make it look like there had been no delay. He swallowed hard knowing they'd give him a hard time and it was truly his fault.

"Damn," he said as he watched the workers make eye contact. Most of them were leaning on the outside of the building, looking bored and irritated. "Let's go. Gotta make up for lost time."

"Okay," Sergio answered back, sensing Lucas's nervousness. "I'll get them started on the back. We're all good."

Lucas quickly looked at him, immediately grateful, and cleared his throat. "Glad we picked you up, Serg. I know a good worker when I see one."

They bumped knuckles and got out of the truck. It was interactions like this that made Lucas miss his brother. After the fight, Tyler moved to Massachusetts to live with their aunt and never set foot in California again. Lucas would never know if it was the intense beating he'd given him that made them lose touch or his strife with The General that did it, but either way, Lucas only had one brother now, and it wasn't the one he wanted. Joseph had turned from a bully to a pushover, and it sickened Lucas to the core.

A little after 11 am, Scotty, Lucas's supervisor pulled up in a new F450. Lucas guessed he'd purchased it with the bonus he'd heard some of the guys had gotten. He hoped to get promoted to supervisor in the next few months. He'd earned it. From what he'd heard it didn't take long.

"You guys know we're knocking this thing down on Friday, right?" Scotty asked, pointing to the wall the guys were working on. "No need to spend too much time on it. Just get what you can out of the thing and then move on." They had been salvaging copper from the walls, and anything else worth value, to use on other projects before it was scheduled to be demolished. Building material costs had skyrocketed, so they were trying to cut corners wherever they could.

Scotty, the supervisor, met eyes with Lucas and walked over to him. "You guys get an early start?" he asked. "Looks good."

"Yeah," Lucas said. "The guys were here a bit early so I thought, hell...let's get to it."

"That's smart. Get this shit done as early as possible and then get out of here."

"You know it."

Lucas knew what it meant to get things done. Although he'd struggled to keep up as a child that was no longer the case. He was the master of his own domain now and wore the power like a medal.

9:25 a.m.

As Leona watched the men step off, the long list of the day came back into focus. She didn't have time for paranoia.

Be here now, she thought.

Although early, the heat caused the fumes of the gasoline-stained streets to waft onto the metro as the doors opened and shut for passengers, making Leona feel ill. Beer and soda cans piled in heaps next to the overfilled trash cans outside the window.

So many people. So much filth. So many broken dreams, she thought. Other parts of Los Angeles were beautiful, but not these streets. No one cared about them.

Fortunately, a happy little boy sat across from her, kicking his feet and listening to some music in his memory that no one else could hear. He was oblivious, and it was beautiful. He was chomping down on a breakfast torta. Her heart fluttered at the sight of his innocence.

An elderly woman, Leona and her friend from McDonalds called Bruja (because of her long grey hair and shabby clothes), sat about ten seats up on the bus. She saw a vibrant rose tattoo on the back of the woman's calf. Leona smiled to herself–she had always liked the woman and thought it funny that they found themselves on the same bus many days although they never spoke to each other. Leona often saw her later at McDonald's when Bruja came in to use the restroom, but the woman never looked at her. Bruja seemed to live on the streets and carried all of her belongings with her. The fact of this inequity sat in Leona's consciousness. The woman had a strange magical look about her though and Leona always wondered if there was more to her.

Luckily Marcus, Leona's manager, was kind enough to let Bruja use the restroom and get water there without making a fuss. He had a soft spot for the underdogs—maybe because he was one himself.

Bruja looked especially sullen as she sat on the bus this morning. It looked like she had suffered a long night. Leona looked her over and wondered about her history. She had dark creases under her eyes.

Maybe I should talk to her, she thought. *Maybe it would make her feel visible.*

She decided against it, being that Bruja never made eye contact with her. It probably meant she wanted to be left alone. Leona directed her gaze back onto the sweet young boy and eavesdropped on him instead–one of her favorite pastimes.

"Do you like your sandwich, mijo?" a woman who seemed to be his grandmother said. She had dark hair and was wearing an oversized muumuu that looked like it was from Hawaii. They were a sweet pair—kind of like bookends on life.

He nodded.

"We're almost there," she said, patting him on the back. He went on eating his sandwich while looking around, a dreamy look on his face. Leona saw an entire meadow of poppies spring up around him instantaneously with swallowtails, larks, and the whole bunch of birds floating in his space. A playful song began to play in the air around her, and for a moment, everything was perfect.

Oh, what a beautiful morning. Oh, what a beautiful day. I've got a wonderful feeling, everything's going my way. There's a bright golden lark in the meadow.

The song her mother used to sing to her in her early years came flooding back to her and she felt a sense of hope, of peace, for the young boy. He had such a wonderful life ahead of him.

She hoped. Maybe he would. Maybe.

Leona always wants the best for everyone. I know this to be true, and it's one of my favorite things about her. She sees it around her and has hope for others, but somehow the face of possibility hides when she looks in the mirror. I struggled with this myself as a young bird, and I wish someone would have come up alongside me and prodded me into self love earlier. So I think to myself, *why continue the cycle?* It's our job to break the negative patterns and forge new pathways for the ones we love. That's my hope. I want to help Leona do this.

"Abuela, what's Mickey Mouse's real name?" the boy inquired, unaffected by the dirty seats, the heat, or anything else based in reality. The Disneyland castle was embroidered on his heavy gray sweatshirt, which was much too hot for the day, but he didn't seem to notice. His chubby legs dangled a few inches above the ground as he kicked. Leona thought it was great that he had no idea how hard life was, and she hoped he would never find out. Maybe something good would happen to him and he'd escape before everything gripped him.

His grandmother laughed. "That's his real name," she said. Then she looked out the window and then sighed—a long, exhausted exhale. The woman looked back at her grandson and repeated, "That's his real name."

"But he's a mouse, so his name is really just Mickey," the boy decided and then went on finishing his breakfast, still kicking his feet up and down. He would meet Mickey one day, most likely, and it would be the best day of his life.

Smart kid, Leona thought. For a moment, she imagined placing a forcefield over the two of them and whisking them away to a different life—one that included amusement parks. She would whirl them up in a cloud, dress them in new and comfortable clothes, fill their bellies with their favorite foods, and set them down gingerly with money in their pockets and a nice home to go to after a long day of fun.

She looked back at him and smiled. He smiled back.

She noticed the pink strings of gum on the bottom of one of his shoes. He was oblivious to it so she decided not to say anything. Why ruin the moment?

All of a sudden, the metro slowed and the passengers shifted forward. She lost her balance and her foot ended up in the same gum that had been haunting him.

"Shit," she muttered, forgetting that a child was across from her.

He scrunched his nose at her to show his disapproval, as she was sure he'd seen his grandmother do to the adults in the house when someone cussed. It caused her to giggle to herself.

"Sorry," she mouthed and smiled.

He seemed to like that and smiled back in forgiveness. "Gum,"he said as he pointed to her shoe, kindly warning her while unaware that it was also on his shoe.

"Yeah, I saw it. Why do people do that?" Leona asked while frowning but then laughed. "Such a bummer, huh?"

"It's so rude," he said like an adult. "They should clean up."

"Yes, they should. You're smart."

"Thank you," he replied, smiling up at his grandmother. She looked at Leona and smiled back at her in gratitude. She was probably thankful that someone was helping to keep her grandson engaged. "My teacher says that to me sometimes."

"That's because it's true," Leona replied.

"Want a bite?" he asked as he held out his half-eaten breakfast, genuinely offering to give it up for her. "You seem hungry."

Leona's heart warmed as she imagined reaching over to take a bite. She was very hungry.

"You're such a good kid!" she said, glowing. "I'm not hungry, but if I was, I'd definitely take you up on that. Plus, I'm about to eat when I get to school."

"You go to school? Me too!" he said. "What grade?"

"I'm in college," she answered, "so I guess grade 14."

"There's a grade 14?" he asked. "Wow!"

"No, not really, but I was just translating years into grades. High school stops at grade 12."

"Oh..." he said, confused, but only caring about the facts for only a fraction of a second.

"You should be proud of him. So sweet!" Leona said to his grandmother. "What a great kid."

He beamed with happiness again as his grandmother draped her arm around his shoulders. "Yes, he's my baby," she said as she planted a kiss on the top of his head.

"I'm not a baby," he interrupted.

The woman laughed as she patted his head. "You're my baby and that will never change."

He looked up at her in irritation at first and then saw her

love glowing back at him. His frown crumbled into a smile. Who could argue with *that*?

As Leona neared her stop, she positioned herself to get off and did so as fast as possible, knowing she had little time. She smiled at the boy and his grandmother. He waved goodbye to her, floppy sandwich in hand.

"See ya," she said. "Have a fun day."

"Bye," he said with his mouth full of warm eggs and soft bread, just as it should be.

Maybe everything will be okay, she thought as she looked back at him and saw him continue to kick his happy feet up in the air.

Gaga

I don't want to be brave; I want to be free.

* * *

When Lady Gaga was brutally assaulted by a music producer at age 19 and then left to deal with an unexpected pregnancy and the shame that came with the attack, she stayed quiet like many other victims do for years after. After she suffered from a psychotic episode years later and ended up in the hospital due to acute pain and numbness, they found that nothing was physically wrong with her and therefore sent her to a psychiatrist who uncovered that she was having recurring PTSD as a response to the rape. She had never confronted her trauma.

According to Gaga, the attack changed her indefinitely, and to this day she has not named the attacker and does not plan to do so. She doesn't want to face him. The rape has caused her tremendous pain and suffering and is still activating at times to this day.

This international super star, with the reputation as a strong and powerful woman, has lived through the trauma that so many women have had to. The number of women who deal with this in their lives is in the billions. It is not rare.

9:32 a.m.

Leona got off at Vermont and hustled past the pizza shop across from campus as the smell of bread wafted through the air. After watching the little boy eat his sandwich, all she could think about was food. The cafeteria was slightly out of the way, so she doubted that she would make it before her class. She had to ignore her needs once again as the time dictated her moves. She could feel the clock ticking; it stops for no one, as we know. It doesn't matter if you're hungry. Leona ran up the linoleum stairs, skipping one here and there, and popped the door open to class just as it was starting.

Professor Langston looked up in her direction and nodded. The professor was a smart and warm black woman, and she seemed to have an affinity for Leona which made her so happy. It felt good to have someone in the higher echelons of education looking out for her. Leona loved Langston's class and felt that each session was like a tiny burst of energy, as she left feeling empowered and more intelligent.

The classroom was full today and most of the students were already seated, taking their laptops out and getting settled in the musty early air. Just like most community college courses, this one was full of a combination of students who didn't want to be there but their parents had forced them to go, others who were just trying to transfer to a university as fast as they could, and few who were in the second or third life, taking classes for the love of learning or to achieve something they hadn't been able to in their younger years. Each student's body language told their story as they either sunk into what they saw as a long class or perked up when Langston stepped to the front.

Sociology was one of the last courses Leona had to take before transferring to a university. She and Carlos had been checking their email constantly since March to see where they'd gotten in and the anticipation was taking a toll on them. He'd been accepted to San Diego State, but he'd have to move there to attend; commuting from L.A. was too much for any sane human. They were hoping to stay together, and so the dream for both of them was UCLA. It was a great school and they wouldn't have to move apart or away from Leona's house, which was cheap, albeit run-down and chaotic. It had taken them about four years to get through community college because they had to work full time and were behind on credits from their lackluster high school experiences.

Leona had applied to multiple schools in Southern California, and she got into UCI, but didn't really want to go there as it seemed too suburban, and she also applied to Loyola, but it was extremely expensive and she'd have to take out substantial loans. This scared her as she didn't know the first thing about managing borrowed money and there was no one to ask because everyone around her was looking to her for leadership.

. . .

Even though I did generally well financially due to my music career, and would call myself smart because I've been reading and learning since I was young, I don't know the first thing about college and couldn't have helped her much despite my desire to do so. When I was around, I tried my best to help with whatever I could, but I didn't know the first thing about how to navigate any of this. It's a world that is sectioned off for the rich and the experienced, and I think it takes a few generations of success to understand the system.

UCLA was the best bet for Leona, as far as she was concerned, being that it would help her make the connections she would need to get into law school. It was her dream. Carlos supported her going there whether he made it in himself, but it didn't mean it wouldn't be painful for them to part. He sometimes joked about her not getting in but she knew he was only truly afraid of his own fate. They had grown so close and being at the same school would feel like a drink of water.

"Nice to see you all," Langston said with a wry smile. "Today we're going to talk about the culture of women and advocacy —women helping women and the issues they face when trying to raise each other up and push against deeply ingrained stereotypes, especially when it comes to the workplace. We'll also discuss how women respond to each other in regards to experiences with assault and harassment."

Immediately, the letter I had written Leona and my other girls about Angela Davis came to Leona's mind and she remembered how Davis once gave a speech about sexual violence. In it she urged women to take a stand against it and confront it instead of ignoring the topic due to the fact that it is taboo.

She expressed that until we do so, nothing would change. I always loved Davis as she was somewhat of a mentor for me, and I think Leona saw her that way as well. I didn't know her–don't get excited–I just read her and then tried my best to soak up her wisdom. Hopefully you have a habit of reading and taking in wisdom from other women, as well. We know so much and can really help one another out if we listen to each other.

"We'll read a bit..." Langston continued, "and then discuss our personal experiences and observations. We'll start with the workplace. To get focused, I'd like you to think about this question: once women move up in their field, do they help each other rise? We'll be looking at multiple case studies in order to come to some conclusions about this."

The class shuffled in their seats, many people were clearly uncomfortable with the topic. Leona was intrigued because she hadn't found women to be as supportive as she wished they were. Her own experience had been less than desirable, as she hadn't seen a lot of them helping each other and it seemed that many times they were in a competition. This was true in most areas of life. She thought of Garcia, her boss at the law office she worked at. She seemed like she put more effort into shoving her heel into other women's necks than giving them a hand up. All she ever heard was judgment—not empathy. It seemed that women in charge rarely gave their female counterparts the benefit of the doubt. Leona hated feeling this way about her gender and hoped that it was an experience that was solely her own, but she doubted it would.

From what she could see it took a lot for women to rise in a field, and it seemed most women wanted others to feel the pain they had to go through in order to get there and sometimes even work hard to prevent other women from ascending. This happened in so many ways from comparisons and judgment to not covering for others. It was not a new concept, but it was a complicated one as well as something that was hush-hush in the world of women. Leona wondered what role she'd played in this. Maybe she'd been a good ambassador for her tribe, or maybe she hadn't. Jolie, a friend from her childhood, was definitely someone she'd felt she'd let down though and she narrowed in on that friendship.

Did she lift her up or push her down?

* * *

When she last saw Jolie, it was a hot spring night, and she'd been walking to JJ's Fried Chicken to get something to eat while thinking about how much she hated her boss. She was in the middle of a mental argument with Garcia in her head—the kind you have when you can't actually tell the person how you feel—when all of the sudden she was interrupted by a yell from the dark side of a brick building far in the distance.

As she drew closer, she saw there was a food line for the unhoused and destitute up against the building. Scores of people were waiting, keeping close tabs on their cherished items. She turned away to continue on her walk. Someone was always yelling regardless of where she was in the city so it didn't strike her as being personal.

"Leo!" She heard the voice again, bellowing from the shadows, and noticed a tall, thin woman with long black dreads jumping up and down excitedly and waving at her. She didn't recognize Jolie at first, a bit taken aback by the fact that someone from the line recognized her. It wasn't until she was about a hundred feet away that she recognized her.

"You blind? It's Jolie," she yelled as she waved Leona over, seemingly confused about the fact that her old friend from high school didn't recognize her immediately.

From what Leona could see, Jolie was a mere shadow of the high school student she had been friends with a few years back. She used to be a beautiful girl—one that all of the guys were trying to connect with—but now she gave off the kind of vibe people shrunk away from. Her energy spoke volumes.

It was obvious that she'd been in one too many hotel rooms over the past few years, and this theory was supported by the way she held herself. Leona's gaze trailed over a tight black T-shirt that was littered with wide seductive holes around the bodice and a purple short skirt that had lost some of its elasticity. Jolie's long legs, still muscular and toned, stood out. She'd always had great legs.

Leona shuddered and then walked closer, and as she did Jolie smiled and tilted her partially-shaved head to the side, showing an ear with piercings top to bottom. She had intensely tired eyes. When they got to each other, however, everything was back to normal and they were as tight as they were in youth. In an instant they were whisked back to high school and Flo Rida's "Low" was blaring as the streets came alive with everyone dancing. It was the perfect kind of party; the type where no one was throwing a drink at anyone and everyone was wrapped up in the love of humanity. Passerbys perked their ears up to the music and stepped into the mix, getting as low to the ground as they could physically muster. It was a game and everyone knew it. Leona and Jolie were young and wild and free again as if nothing could ever go wrong and the world was at their fingertips. Jolie's huge smile and shining white teeth lit up and Leona smiled in response to her friend's happiness. They were two birds on a wire.

Jolie had been the only girl who was decent to Leona when she had first moved back to L.A. in the middle of her freshman year. On her second day in Mr. Wilken's algebra class, she leaned over quietly and asked if she could borrow a pencil.

"Uh, yeah, sure," Leona responded in haste and handed it to her, not knowing if Jolie was of the kind or cruel variety. She remembered thinking she looked popular.

Jolie looked back at her with a wide grin. "You're new, right? I haven't seen you before." Her braids hung down around her face in a way that made her look younger than she was, but she had an old soul essence because she dressed like a hippie.

"Well, I'm from L.A., but we moved away for a few years, so yeah, I guess I'm new again," she said. "We used to live in Silver Lake."

"My aunt lives there. You must be rich," she said, smiling with glowing white teeth. "Why didn't you move back there? I hate to break it to you, but it's not nice here," she said with a laugh.

"Yeah, I noticed. We lived at my grandma's back then, but she sold the place a while ago, so now we're here," Leona answered reluctantly. "I was down in O.C. for the last few years. It's different down there."

"I thought you said you weren't rich," Jolie said, smiling and raising her eyebrows. "Must be nice. You have a horse? I can see you out riding with your long braids blowing in the wind."

"Do I really look like I have a horse?" Leona laughed. She'd never been called rich before. Where she had lived she'd been low income.

"I mean, kinda..." Jolie said and hit her arm. They became instant friends.

The food line Jolie was in moved up, and Leona thought about how much they had changed. A worn-out young woman had taken her friend's place. It saddened her deeply and she suddenly wanted to save her.

"Sorry," she said as she pulled away. "I couldn't see who you were from back there. I think I need glasses."

"Yeah, I guess so. I can't believe it's you!" Jolie cried in joy as she released her from her tight embrace. "How long has it been?" she asked as she moved herself back so as to make sure not to lose her spot in line. Jolie was entirely focused on eating, it seemed. Leona wondered how long she'd been doing all of this begging. Her friend looked desperate.

"Not sure..." Leona said as she took her friend in. One of Jolie's previously stunning white teeth was chipped and her skin had taken on the appearance of an overripe plum.

Leona struggled to act normal after noticing how bad things were. The longer she stood there the more she noticed. *How did things get so bad so quickly?* she thought. She always assumed Jolie would come out on top. She just had that energy, the good kind of energy that thrives and overcomes all odds. It seemed she had been mistaken.

"So...how are you?" she asked, trying to ignore the obvious. She instantly regretted the question, feeling as if it made things more solid.

The line moved forward and a man behind her huffed loudly as he tried to lift a leg that seemed to want to stay put. A few people behind them, an elderly man who was missing half of his shirt, had a foul smell leaking from him and was rocking back and forth as he waited impatiently.

It seemed Jolie had hit rock bottom.

"I mean, things have been hard, as you can see. I wouldn't be *here* if they hadn't. No one wants to do this," she said as she held her arm out to emphasize the line. "But I'm making it...I think. I just don't know..." The last word rolled out of her mouth like a marble, helplessly following the line of gravity. Her eyes shot downward.

An awkward silence sat between them as the line moved up again. Some grumbling could be heard from behind them again; it seemed someone thought that Leona was going to cut in line. She looked back and motioned that she wasn't going to take anyone's place. Hungry eyes stared back at her.

"That's good. ...I mean, it's good you're doing okay. I haven't seen you since..." The longer they talked, the more she could see that Jolie was high on something. Her eyes were bloodshot, and she trembled slightly. With multiple tattoos on her arms and legs, it was tough to imagine that her road hadn't resulted in a few dead ends.

Leona's heart sank more and more as she continued taking her in. "...I think it was at Joe's house last..."

"Yeah, yeah. I think so. Sorry I dropped off the face of the planet. I got myself into some trouble after I started hanging with Johnny. He was so crazy-cool back then. Always doing what he wanted—nobody owned him. I respected that." She looked down at the asphalt. "I really thought he was going to be something. ...well, he turned out to be something, alright—an asshole."

"I'm sorry, girl. I'm sorry," Leona responded as she glanced at Jolie's sad eyes and grabbed her for another hug. "I'm sure you're on your way up though, right?"

"Nowhere to go but up," Jolie said as she fell into a self-diminishing laugh. "I'm living at a friend's right now, trying to find a job, but no one will hire me because I got locked up," she said casually. Leona had heard something about her stint in prison but had forgotten about it.

"What happened with that?"

"Well, after the rape, I lost myself and messed everything up. Remember that? I had no idea it wasn't my fault, so I took it out on myself. I screwed around with everyone and made myself pay for it. I felt that somehow I had asked for it."

At that moment, Leona remembered how much they had

in common. Jolie had been with her right before her own life fell apart and soon after, Jolie followed suit.

* * *

As she thought about Jolie and her attack, she remembered that she hadn't known how to help her at the time. She remembered wishing she could give her an exoskeleton to wear so she could slip it on whenever she felt that she was in danger and never have to worry again. It wouldn't matter how much a man tried to force themselves into a woman then, they would be prevented from entering. And maybe the exoskeleton could also have electrical impulses so that the man would be flung far away from her body. *Yes*, Leona thought. *All women need this.* The very thought of this requirement was pathetic in her mind though. It shouldn't take great engineering to make men stop assaulting women. The concept was much too complicated to end there anyway. No one knows what could actually prevent these attacks. No one except the men who had choose to rape; they themselves are the only ones who could put a stop to this crime.

The decision lies in their hands, but how do you tame a beast?

To them, women are like dust floating in the sunlight, aimlessly falling to the dirty carpet and straight into the palm of the oppressor.

* * *

Leona remembered meeting eyes with Jolie after her friend had admitted being sexually assaulted.

Leona had said she was so sorry that had happened to her, but she'd always carried guilt about not doing more to help her friend. Not only did she neglect to help her, she had also refrained from telling Jolie about her own attack. It seemed too fresh and somehow pointless at the time. Neither person had done what the other needed and that seemed typical—almost unavoidable. It was something she thought women needed to get better at.

Jolie brushed it off as if it was nothing. "I got pretty screwed up, I guess. I just started doing things. Things I wasn't proud of."

"I wish I would have done more for you," Leona said in regret. "I didn't realize that it affected you so much, but I should have. Of course it did. I was such an idiot."

"We were kids, Leona. There's no blame there," Jolie said with softness in her voice, trying to remove any guilt Leona had. "I didn't talk about it much. I think I was in denial, you know?"

"Yeah, I get it," she responded. They were two peas in a rotten pod.

"Can I ask you a question?" Jolie said suddenly, noticing Leona's concerned look.

"Yeah, shoot," she said.

"I always wondered why you seemed so paranoid back then. Why was that? You were always so worried, especially when the guys came around."

Leona paused for a second. She wondered if she should mention that she had also been attacked. She had never told Jolie when they were younger because she was trying to keep it down, stuck in the chasm of her consciousness. Maybe it would make more sense to Jolie if she did. Maybe it would excuse her inaction. Her stomach grumbled, and she began to feel dizzy again but then did nothing. *It was nine years ago,* she thought. *Too much time has passed.*

"Oh, I don't know," Leona answered. "I just had a lot going on at that time, I guess."

"Hmm...okay. Just wondering. I always thought maybe..."

Suddenly Leona had an urgent desire to leave. This was a past she didn't want to bring up. It was happier lying in its grave. "I've got to go, Jo," Leona said, quickly cutting her off to avoid any more questions. "It was so nice to see you, though, and I hope things get better soon."

Jolie seemed taken back by her harsh abruptness for a moment, but then she moved solidly back into the food line. She quickly shifted back into the pattern of superficial civility and Leona recognized it, thankful for the facade because it released her from the intensity of the conversation.

"Next time I see you, I'll be into something good, I promise," Jolie continued. "I'll be driving a BMW blasting 'Pony' or something like that. Ha! Remember how much we loved that song?"

"Oh my God, yeah. Funny thing is I had no idea what it was about back then."

"You always were the innocent one," Jolie said with a smile.

* * *

"...you've experienced, Leona?" was all she heard when she was shaken out of her long reflection by Professor Langston.

Because Leona's mind was usually engaged in the discussions in class and most of the time deeply intrigued in the topics as well, her professor most likely assumed that she had been analyzing the topic at hand. This time, she had not been though, and because of this she found herself completely lost.

"Um..." Leona muttered. "Uh." She sat up in her seat and tried to regain awareness as her hands grew clammy. "Would you be so kind as to rephrase the question? I want to make sure I completely understand what you're asking," she said, trying to buy time. "I was a bit distracted."

"Sure, not a problem," Langston responded, laughing

lightly as she realized she'd caught Leona off guard. "From your perspective and the readings, do you believe that women back each other up when it comes to providing support for victims of sexual harassment and assault?"

Her guilt about not being there for Jolie grew feet after hearing the question. *No, they do not,* she thought. Even *she* hadn't done what she now wished she had when Jolie had spilled the details of her assault. She'd let Jolie cry on her shoulder as she silently listened and that was about the extent of her "support."

Leona took a deep breath and gathered her thoughts before answering. *Should she be honest or just say what everyone wanted to hear?* It seemed that most women didn't really help other women much; that's what she knew to be true. At times she found herself speaking truth to fiction, but whenever she said something about this misalignment of sorts, the claws came out. It was an unwritten norm that women wouldn't admit.

Whenever Leona brought it up, the onus of responsibility was put on her. *Well, maybe* you *don't support other women, but* I *do,* is what they always seemed to say. To her, women seemed to be competitive rather than supportive. She always wondered if they were taught to be that way because of the enormously high standards placed upon them or if it was due to something more biological—perhaps vying for the best mate? Maybe it was a hunter-gatherer thing? Either way, assault was an experience that plagued many of them and when someone admitted it, many women brushed it off, or simply said, "how sad" or "hmm...me too." It was rare that they stood up for each other or actually helped each other through it, especially if men were around.

. . .

"I mean..." Leona paused, thinking about how to say what she had to say in a way that would pave a new path instead of opening wounds. "...when I've talked about this with friends —some of whom have dealt with assault themselves—it has seemed like most people want to push it away—like it will disappear if we just stay quiet or ignore it. This obviously doesn't work. A lot of us just keep our trauma to ourselves, but when we do talk about it, I would have to say there isn't a lot of support. It's more discomfort, and sometimes even apathy, we receive."

She paused, realizing that she had basically admitted that she had been assaulted. "So no, I'd say that from my experience, we don't support each other like we need to when it comes to rape. If anything, we make things worse by ignoring it or just saying it's so common," she said as she looked around and noticed that everyone was staring at her. "Our responses are kind of crazy though. If someone has been attacked, they need help, not criticism or silence, and they need to be vindicated for the harm that was done to them. Honestly, I think they have a right to take revenge. Most people don't seem to get how hard it is to carry this type of emotional load. I wish they did, but they don't. It's not the same as a punch in the gut. It takes a toll on your mind and body. I admit that I've been part of the problem. I wish it wasn't true, but I have been less than helpful when my friends have talked about men touching them or forcing them into things. I'm learning, though. I hope we're all learning. One thing I do know is that we can't sit in silence anymore. That's for sure. We should fight back."

The tension stood constipated in the small, stuffy room. It was suddenly quiet as if Leona had cursed Langston out or disrupted the flow of energy that existed before she spoke. Something was out of place and she couldn't figure it out. A boat had been rocked.

. . .

My tiny heart burst with pride as Leona sat there surprised by her audacity to say exactly what she was thinking and what everyone needed to hear. It was a bit blunt, but so necessary.

I have to say I saw it coming too–this metamorphosis in her–Leona had been growing for days and it seemed this morning was a special one. I'm not sure why, but I did know something would happen. I could hear it in the leaves.

You see, I have watched Leona since she was a twig and although her roots had been driven over like a teenager in a jeep she was building thick skin. It was beautiful, and I knew it was exactly what she needed.

From afar I saw her sit up confidently in her chair while she wondered who she was becoming. She looked a little bit like what I imagine Joan of Arc would have looked like in the moment of fire, or maybe America Ferrera when she did that interview and dismissed naysayers, or maybe even Alexandria Ocasio-Cortez when she stood up for the working class and told it how it was. All in all, she looked like someone who was proud of who she was and unafraid to fight the good fight. I wasn't quite sure she'd expressed the best sentiment regarding revenge, however––violence doesn't solve violence–but I was impressed to see her stand up for herself and other women. She was finding her voice.

Leona classmates stared at her in awe. Some seemed to be shooting little darts at her head like a spontaneously crafted array of tiny energetic needles. *Why did you shake things up?* While others just stared. The earth shook and laptops shifted. Some throats were cleared in interest or disgust–she couldn't tell at the moment–and suddenly she wondered if someone had said something in contrast to her while she had been stuck in her Jolie nostalgia and unaware of the conversation.

"What are we supposed to do, talk about it for the rest of

our lives?" a tall brunette with a red Texas A&M t-shirt on blurted out, shattering the silence that filled the room. "Like I said before your little speech, women do support each other. I mean, maybe *you* don't support your friends, but I know *I* do. What's there left to do? Things are so much better now. I don't know why everyone is always complaining about everything. Maybe you just need to grow some," she said, leaning towards her boyfriend, who looked to be a harasser. His tousled brown hair bounced as he looked at her with haughty, hungry green eyes. 'That's my girl,' Leona imagined him saying.

And then to Leona's dismay, the woman continued. "Sure, sometimes people are assaulted, but a lot of that can be avoided if we just watch where we are and be careful about what we're wearing," she continued. There was audible silence. Breathing took effort, as the tension sat fiercely. "It's not that big of a deal, but when it happens we've got each other's backs. I know I love my girls, and we always help each other out."

Leona was taken aback. It was evident that she'd committed a social faux pas while daydreaming, but she was floored by the fact that the woman had essentially blamed the victim and their choice of clothing when it came to harassment. She also didn't believe her claim of being super supportive. It just didn't seem likely.

She could not let the comments sit still. This was exactly the problem they were discussing and the woman had come at her, feisty and all, instead of trying to join with her or make the contrast in a kind and supportive way.

The class sat silent until a man cut the tension by laughing a nervous laugh, or maybe it was scoffing, Leona didn't know which. A few people rolled their eyes while some nodded in agreement, and she felt a fierce anger building inside of her. For a moment she didn't know what to do. It seemed she'd awakened the beast inside of her and it was now at her feet waiting to be fed.

All day there had been a silent rumbling in her belly and in this moment, she felt alive. She decided she'd had enough but, just when she thought nothing could provoke her further, the woman continued, "*Some* people just can't deal." She pursed her colored lips like a model as she stretched her long legs in front of her and basked in the light. "I guess you just have to be tough."

These were fighting words and although Leona was determined not to become the woman's nemesis, it was futile. Her body rebelled as her mind tried to contain it. Fists flung themselves into the ring and she stood face to face with the ignorant paper doll woman. Her eyes seemed to be welcoming the fight. The bell rang and the crowd roared as they shook their fists in the air. *Who will win: the beauty in the right corner? She's got the body of a gazelle and doesn't look a day past 21. Or the waif of a woman? She's short and stocky, but fierce like a snake.* Everyone placed their bets and Leona grabbed the key to harness its power once more before completing what she hoped to be a total knockout.

She didn't want to be part of the exact problem they had been discussing in class, but her belly growled for the fight. She went in for the kill despite her rational mind's begging.

"Are you serious? You're saying you don't have guys cat-calling you while you're walking down the street? That assault doesn't seem to happen any more? That rape isn't really a problem? What the fuck is wrong with you? Are you honestly that stupid?"

"Don't call me stupid," the brunette said, rolling her eyes. "I don't know but it's not a big deal to me. I take it as a compliment," she paused and the class shuffled wide eyed. Her boyfriend smiled at her as if to congratulate her. "It's only a problem if you let it get to you. Maybe you should try it sometime or maybe you don't get much attention. Maybe that's your real issue."

"Basta!" Leona yelled and stood up. The class stared at her, wondering what was about to happen.

The brunette laughed a bit and took a stand herself, towering over Leona. "What?" she said. "Speak English. I don't know what you're saying."

"Yeah, you don't. You...racist idiot. It means 'enough.' You're part of the problem, you know? You and women like you. You're the reason we're in the predicament we're in with your ignorant little 'everything's fine' attitude and your pandering to the men around you. It's sick. This is why men still rape and get away with it. They know there are people like you who will shut up and take it."

The boyfriend suddenly burst into laughter and hearing this, the brunette turned to shush him. "Be quiet," she said and then whispered, "You're embarrassing." She directed her attention back to Leona and quietly said, "I'm just saying we need to get over it."

"She's just a stupid feminist," the boyfriend said under his breath and leaned back in complete comfort. "Who cares what she says."

The class sat in awe as Leona and the brunette stared at each other.

Langston stood still and quiet at the front of the room, seemingly unsure about what to do. She looked at the two of them, but focused on Leona. Her silent presence was powerful and helped Leona to steady herself.

"Okay, okay. That's enough," she said sternly. "Go ahead and take your seats. We've got to keep things civil. This won't solve anything. In fact, it's interesting because it's an exact example of the topic at hand. Now, let's get back to having a calm discussion. This time, without the insults," she said as she looked at Leona.

Leona's stomach was still churning and she had a fierce desire to destroy the brunette, but she managed to sit down. She knew she could win too, but she had to stop. It wasn't the woman's fault she was so ignorant. The entire society yelled "shut up and ignore it" when it came to rape and she was just a victim of her culture. At that moment, Leona remembered what I had always told her: "Be like water. As the waves come, flow with them. Don't fight against something that will not move. Flow around it and get it done."

"Okay, I am contemplating your position, and I'm sorry for calling you stupid. I see, you think we can ignore it," Leona said, "but that is exactly my point. Instead of trying to effect real change in our society by talking about these issues and supporting each other when bad things happen, it's easier to push things aside and pretend that everything is fine, but that is exactly what the perpetrators want: silence. Nothing—and I mean *nothing*—changes if we do that. The cycle continues generation after generation as it has for thousands of years. A predator and his prey. But when the prey learns to defend herself either physically or in terms of legislation, the monsters begin to hide. They no longer feel comfortable to yell on the streets or grab people and rape them in the alleys or on college campuses. They need to know that there are consequences, but this can only happen if we band together. It takes all of us. We need to fight back."

Leona was on stage, and she knew it. The claps and guffaws were rolling in. All eyes were fixed on her, and it was good, making her feel alive, whether it was dangerous or not. In this moment, her voice did not waver.

The brunette laughed as she looked around and found herself at a loss for words. Her boyfriend's hand was on her neck, caressing it lightly. *Just a little more, baby. Keep it up.* It seemed he pulled the strings as she danced. Generations of marionettes pulled their puppets up and down.

Leona decided to make a final remark after witnessing the manipulation. "We sat in silence when we needed to yell. I think it's time to yell now."

A few people cleared their throats and stared in awe. Most of them sat there quietly, but given the look on their faces, Leona knew she had gotten them stirring.

The brunette looked away for a moment, defeated and seemingly embarrassed, before leaning back and whispering something in her boyfriend's ear. He laughed and caressed her neck.

"Yeah, I guess..." she finally muttered halfheartedly towards Leona. "I mean, when you put it that way, all emotional and stuff, it makes everyone feel like it's an issue whether it is or not."

Leona felt her blood pressure rising, but then stopped the escalation. It was useless. The brunette was past the point of reason, or reflection: she was knee deep in taboos. There would be no changing this for her. Not today. Maybe not ever.

"Well, rape is emotional, yes, and I'm sorry but I'd have to say that I just disagree. I think this is an issue for everyone," Leona said.

Professor Langston nodded in Leona's direction. "Okay, thank you. It seems like there is a lot to be said on this, and I'm glad we've had an honest discussion. Listening is the first step toward understanding and understanding is the first step toward growth." She paused. "Please read 'We Should All Be Feminists' by Adichie by Thursday. We will continue this discussion then. I'm looking forward to hearing what you think about this short piece."

The class shuffled their belongings and began to exit quickly. At this, the brunette looked over at Leona and smirked as she stood up. She was tall and voluptuous, with long brown hair, fake eyelashes, and thick lips. Leona knew the woman had been harassed her entire life. She wondered what she thought about all of this when she was alone—or even when she was lying in bed at night next to her boyfriend. She wondered if she slept well.

The woman's boyfriend joined her in standing and chuckled in arrogance in Leona's direction as he walked outside. He seemed to be the type to have a hyper masculine YouTube channel and struck her as a leader among young men, showing them how to be more violent. *I'm alpha*, she imagined him saying. She wondered about his relationship with his mother. Where were the mothers of these guys?

"Feminist," he mouthed at Leona, as if it were an insult, and shook his head. His girlfriend laughed and touched his arm lightly, trying to pull him along. She was obviously uncomfortable with how far things had gone; it looked as if she were used to nudging her boyfriend away from chaotic situations. She had spoken, but he was the speaker.

Leona glared at him confidently and noticed that for the first time, she didn't feel dizzy when facing a guy of this nature. It was a feat for her. Something had shifted. She'd admitted her rape and was strong enough to face everything, even if others were uncomfortable.

The boyfriend looked once more at her, eyeing her up and down, and then walked out, tapping the side of the door frame audibly as if to show his ownership of everything he came into contact with. He was exactly the type who would call her out on the street, and his girlfriend was exactly the type who would stay quiet about it—a never-ending cycle with multiple parties involved.

The Rapist is You

I don't want to be brave; I want to be free.

* * *

In 2019, on International Day for the Elimination of Violence Against Women, hundreds women came together outside the Supreme Court in Santiago, Chile to protest against harassment and assault.

In unison, and in blindfolds, they chanted the song "Un Violador en Tu Camino," an anthem written by Las Tesis as a response to the fact that sexual abuse is common in Chile and less than 10% of rapes yield convictions.

Many of the protestors viewed the courts as an arm of the patriarchy rather than an entity that protected them against the violence that had become normalized in their society.

This anthem for solidarity among women against sexual violence spread to cities around the world (Bogota, New York, Paris, etc) where women used it to protest against violence and victim-blaming and to bring awareness to how common violence is.

The problem persists today.

"Un Violador en Tu Camino"
by Las Tesis

El patriarcado es un juez
que nos juzga por nacer,
y nuestro castigo
es la violencia que no ves.
El patriarcado es un juez
que nos juzga por nacer,
y nuestro castigo
es la violencia que ya ves.
Es feminicidio.
Impunidad para mi asesino.
Es la desaparición.
Es la violación.
Y la culpa no era mía, ni dónde estaba ni cómo vestía.
Y la culpa no era mía, ni dónde estaba ni cómo vestía.
Y la culpa no era mía, ni dónde estaba ni cómo vestía.
Y la culpa no era mía, ni dónde estaba ni cómo vestía.
El violador eras tú,
El violador eres tú.
Son los pacos,
los jueces,
el Estado,
el presidente.
El Estado opresor es un macho violador
El Estado opresor es un macho violador
El violador eras tú.
El violador eres tú.
Duerme tranquila, niña inocente
sin preocuparte del bandolero,
que por tu sueño dulce y sonriente

vela tu amante carabinero.
El violador eres tú.
El violador eres tú.
El violador eres tú.
El violador eres tú.

"A Rapist In Your Path"
by Las Tesis
(*Translated from Spanish*)
Patriarchy is a judge
that judges us for being born,
our punishment
is the violence you don't see.
Patriarchy is a judge
that judges us for being born,
our punishment
is the violence you now see.
It's femicide,
Impunity for my killer.
It's disappearance.
It's rape.
And it's not my fault, nor where I was, nor what I wore.
And it's not my fault, nor where I was, nor what I wore.
And it's not my fault, nor where I was, nor what I wore.
And it's not my fault, nor where I was, nor what I wore.
The rapist was you
The rapist is you.
It's policemen,
Judges,
The state,
The president.
The oppressive state is a rapist.
The oppressive state is a rapist.
The oppressive state is a rapist.

The oppressive state is a rapist.
The rapist was you
The rapist is you.
Sleep tight, innocent girl
don't worry about the criminal,
your policeman lover is taking care
of your sweet dreams.
The rapist is you.
The rapist is you.
The rapist is you.
The rapist is you.

11:32 a.m.

As Leona gathered her things to go, a tall blonde woman in her forties with a tie dyed tank top on, approached her.

"That was awesome." Leona looked up anxiously. She hadn't expected anyone to talk to her after her argument. The woman continued, "I wanted to say thank you," she said as she looked at Leona "I've been annoyed with that crazy woman for the last few weeks. She's always spouting out some sort of nonsense, and it's usually something self-deprecating. Does she not get it? She's hurting us all."

"I don't think so," Leona replied as she laughed and found herself happy that she seemed to have an ally. "She was definitely unaware of the truth or unable to speak it. Either way, it was irritating and counter-productive."

"I know. I'm glad you said something. More people need to be brave, like you."

"That's funny, I always say I don't want to be brave; I want to be free."

"Well, maybe freedom is bravery?" the woman questioned.

"I mean if we are brave, freedom will follow. It seems to be the only way it ever unfolds.

At this, Leona felt a huge lump develop in her throat. She didn't want this statement to be true. She wanted to be free without having to stick her neck out. It was so tiring. Before she could catch herself, tears welled up in her eyes and then fell to her cheeks. The woman noticed and leaned forward in response.

"I'm so sorry...I didn't mean to make you upset," she said and reached out to give Leona a hug.

As she fell into the woman's embrace, Leona tried to get a hold of herself for a moment, but instead she allowed herself to be vulnerable. She was tired of doing it alone.

"It's okay," Leona responded. "You didn't do it. It's not you. I'm so sorry. So sorry. We just met too. How uncomfortable." She rubbed her eyes and tried to speak as if nothing was wrong. "I'm just so tired of fighting, especially with women. Shouldn't we all be on the same side?"

"Yes, we should and don't worry about me. I'm an old lady, and I'm happy to help. I know what you're going through. I was raped too, and honestly, no one really listened. Seems it's too common for anyone to bat an eye. We really need to lift each other up. I'm glad you took a stand today."

"I'm so sorry that happened to you, and thank you so much," Leona said as she straightened herself up, wiped her eyes, and stepped back. "Me too. That's why I'm so passionate about it. I had never admitted it to anyone in public before though, and I think the intensity is settling in. I really need to go to therapy. I guess my boyfriend was right," she said with a lighthearted laugh. "I hate it when that happens."

"Me too," the woman responded. "It's rare, but sometimes they are right."

"You're a cool person," Leona responded. "Thank you for

encouraging me. I truly appreciate it. And you're not old, by the way. I hope you know that."

"You're pretty cool yourself, Leona. And just remember, you're not alone in this. We're all in it together. Well, I guess not all of us as you saw," she admitted, referring to what had just happened, "...but many of us are. We will win, even if it takes decades."

11:34 a.m.

Scotty had a way about him, one that Lucas envied. He was confident without coming off as a small guy with a Napoleon complex, despite his short stature, and the others listened to him. It was no wonder he became a supervisor so quickly. From what he'd heard Scotty had been on the job less than a year when he rose to become buddies with the construction manager. He heard they went out to see the Dodgers on weekends and hung out at the CEO's place in Glendale. There was nothing Lucas wanted more than this–a ticket to the show he felt he'd been kept out of the party all of his life.

"You guys up for tacos?" Scotty asked Sergio and Lucas as they finished loading the dumpster with debris. "I'm buying."

Of course he's buying, thought Lucas. *He always has to show off.* He admired it though. He wanted to be able to do the same. Someday maybe he would.

"Yeah, tacos sound great. I'll tell Serg," Lucas said as he

ripped an old piece of PCV pipe out of the wall next to him. Everything had to go, that was part of the reason he loved the job. Their job was to rip everything apart. He was an expert at that.

As they walked over to a bustling street stand, Lucas jogged up alongside Scotty, who walked at a New York pace. "So what's up for tonight? Think we can get out of here early?" Sergio trailed behind.

"Looks that way," he said. "Want to go pound some down afterwards? It seems like that type of night. My woman has been such a pain in the ass lately. Where you going? What are you doing? Blah Blah Blah...I want more. I just need to get away."

"I'm down," Lucas responded. "I'm always up for a few drinks. I'll have to drop Sergio off first, but then we can meet up."

"Yeah, that guy is a downer."

"Tell me about it," Lucas responded as he walked faster, making sure Sergio couldn't hear. "All he ever talks about is his family. My wife this, my daughters that..."

"He's pussy whipped," Scotty replied with a laugh. "You won't catch me like that. My girls know what's up. They know who their daddy is."

"Same. I'm not into that girl boss shit," Lucas said and looked back to motion Sergio over to the stand they'd chosen.

Lucas had been careful not to let Sergio hear his slight. As he looked back he could see that Sergio was in a world of his own. He wondered what kept him going; his life looked so pathetic. More and more, he noticed men cowering to their wives and girlfriends and it pissed him off.

There was a lot of chatter about "taking things back" online and he'd found it enlightening. He hadn't known that women were once men's property in America–thanks to his lackluster high school education which didn't mention much about women's rights besides the fact that they had to fight to get the right to vote–and the fact of how things once were, energized him. It seemed right that men would lead. Of course women shouldn't be on their own, make their own choices, they need men to guide them, he found himself thinking. He found cells of men online who talked about this all day. He felt they got him. Xcel24 had mentioned that he told his girlfriend "no" when she said she was going to go out with her friends and instead of fighting back she just gave in.

That bitch just buckled. I didn't know it was that easy. Just tell them how it will be and they'll do it. They know what's what. They've gotten too much power, so they falsely think they have it.

And there was another post he really liked:

Bgdyxxx wrote: *Stupid bitch just stayed after I beat the shit out of her. Serves her right. Glad she knows her place. You just got to strangle them into submission. You'll see, they'll submit.*

All of this made sense to Lucas. He was glad there were other guys like him online. He didn't know many of them in person, but their virtual presence was strong. There were even some women who seemed to subscribe to the idea they held. Some seemed to want men to "be men" and show their dominance. It was a subculture, as far as he was concerned, and he felt he'd found himself a home.

He thought of some of his old friends who had understood him. They used to have so much fun, Vlad, Georgie, and him, back in high school. Back before everything changed they used to run the streets and pick up all types of women. Vlad was his favorite because he had no fear. Nothing was off limits and no one had a chance against him. He'd been courageous because he'd been through so much, coming from Russia at a time when everything had begun to fall apart, and because of this he feared nothing. Lucas always respected him. As far as he was concerned, he understood what it meant to be a man.

But Vlad and Georgie were long gone, in jail and on drugs, respectively, so he found himself alone in his quest to regain dominance. That is, until he found his place online. Every night he went home and engaged in these chat rooms and listened to these guy's podcasts. His favorite was about taking the home back. So many guys interacted on the show. It seemed like everyone was on his side–but in secret. He wondered why they seemed afraid to say things in public. They mostly spoke under the protection of anonymity, but he knew some day they'd stand up and take what was theirs. It was only a matter of time.

The heat emanated from the sidewalk as Lucas, Scotty, and Sergio lined up behind hungry patrons. The smell of al pastor and carne asada wafted through the air as their stomachs growled.

Once they got in line, Sergio distanced himself again. Lucas and Scotty seemed to think they were superior to him, and it sickened him. Because of this, he found himself wishing he was back at the job site with the day laborers. They were better people. If he didn't want the free lunch, he never would have joined them, but money was tight. They were trying to save to put their oldest in preschool and the tuition was expensive.

He stood behind them, looking at his phone and then suddenly saw a message from his wife. *Things are okay,* he thought. *Even though I have to deal with these assholes, my life is good.* His wife had sent him a text of his oldest daughter playing on the playground at the park near their house. She'd made it down the slide without crying for the first time. They had worked all weekend on this feat, so the success felt huge. A paleta here, a sticker there. All to learn to be unafraid. It was beautiful.

The text read: *Small victory.*

He answered back: *mi corazon.*

11:38 a.m.

Leona felt better, but the fight seemed to have accelerated her starvation. She was hungry in so many ways. She needed to eat. As she moved to the cafeteria she considered the argument she just had wasn't sure how she felt about it. *Was that a win? Did she awaken anyone? Did it do more harm than good? It was hard to know.*

The cafeteria was a ghost town. Rickety chairs sat next to empty tables—quite an unusual sight like the aftermath of an alien invasion. Leona assumed that most students had probably already used their funds for the month. She considered poverty as she peered into the refrigerator. It was stocked with a decent selection of sandwiches and snacks. She rapidly chose a turkey and cheese sandwich and some chips and darted to the checkout line.

The sandwich was cold in her hands, and she was tempted to rip the plastic right open and sink her hungry teeth into it before moving forward but there was no time. She would have to eat on the bus because the minutes had vanished, as usual. She threw everything into her bag and hustled down the stairs.

. . .

The bus pulled up right as she reached the stop. She was out of breath and sweaty. It was the lunch rush hour, so she had to make her way past everyone to try to find a seat once she got on. It seemed that most people were trying to grab a quick lunch, so every seat was taken by someone with food in their hands. She wanted to be eating too, but there was nowhere to sit. The pole in the middle of the car was her best bet.

The ride to Garcia and Stevens was twenty minutes on good days and longer on busy ones. Once she got there she wouldn't be able to eat so this was her only chance. A frantic energy took hold of her and her hunger screamed out. She imagined herself as a gigantic vulture-like bird with the wingspan of a car. She often thought of herself as some type of bird, or rather wished she was one, because it seemed to her they had more control of their lives and were more able to escape danger than she was. If she was one she could soar downtown, tuck in her wings, spin a few times, and then be back in her human body in time for work. The reality was that she was the human variety of flesh and bones and had no way to soar above anything. She was stuck in the grid just like everyone else.

I wished I could tell her what was to come, wished I could whisk her away. It seemed she was learning her way though. My chest burst with pride in this realization.

Garcia rushed into Leona's mind. Her boss ruffled the feathers of even the most sleek of her peers and nobody ever knew what to expect when she was around. If she was there, everyone held their breath until she stopped circling. Stevens was more relaxed, but he wasn't usually in the office. He was a luxury lawyer, as they put it—one who didn't really need to win cases anymore. According to rumor, he was a trust fund baby who did law for fun and was really only good at getting clients. Garcia was the hound who won everything she got her hands on, but did it with a toxic fire in her belly and a lot of collateral damage among her staff

Garcia had come up on her own and pushed mountains to get to where she was and wanted everyone to know about it. Leona respected her journey, but she hated working for her. She was a terror. You have to be steely and jaded to bulldoze people. That harshness comes from somewhere. As Leona saw it, it must be a response to force, but she still could have mercy on her coworkers. It seemed Garcia wanted everyone to work as hard as she had.

Leona watched a man leave his seat on the bus and rushed to take his spot. She sat down in the roughly carpeted seat next to the side door, as exhaust blew in from under the entryway, and fumbled to get her sandwich. Her phone was in the way so she instinctively grabbed it instead. Carlos had texted her:

Call me.

She put off hunger for a minute longer.

"Hey, Los! What's up? I'm on the bus, and it's hard to hear. Need something?" she asked.

"I didn't get in," he said. "I just got the email."

The silence sat like a ghost.

"To UCLA?..." The pause lingered as her image of a perfect exit for the two of them faded. Their silence acknowledged the small defeat, and Leona instantaneously found herself questioning her desire to go on without him.

"Yeah, I didn't think I'd make it, honestly," Carlos continued. He was always self-deprecating. He was really intelligent, and Leona wanted him to know how competent he was. He lost sight of it sometimes. Some of his insecurity bled into passive aggression at times, and she couldn't blame him, but she didn't like it.

"Don't say that. You're amazing. You know it's a numbers game. I probably won't get in either."

"Yeah, probably not," he said in a slight slump, but then he caught himself. "No, just kidding, Ona. You will. You deserve it."

"But you do too. Deserving something has nothing to do with what happens. We all know that."

"You'll get in. You're a much better student than me."

"Oh my god, stop it," she paused. "I don't know if I even want to anymore. I don't really want to do it without you."

"Please...that's enough," he responded. "You will get in, and we'll be fine. Nothing is going to end us. Plus, I didn't really want to be with you anyways."

"Ha ha."

"Really though...you'll get in and you'll go. You've worked so hard for this and I'd never stop you."

"It's not like you could anyways," Leona said, trying to lighten his sad mood.

"True. So true," he said.

She didn't want to consider living the next few years without a daily dose of Carlos. They had built each other up, and it made everything seem worth it; all of the hardship had less of an edge with him. She knew their relationship would stand the test of time no matter what, but absence was something neither of them wanted.

"Love you," she said.

"You too," he responded.

Her low spirits lingered as she hung up and looked out the window. The idea of long days without him unfolded in front of her, and everything looked darker. All her silly superstitious promises to every possible entity in hopes of securing spots for the both of them at their dream school hadn't worked. This wasn't unexpected, though. God had been quiet all of her life. The idea of a higher power who loved you was a fantasy that some old men made up to explain the unexpected and garner power along the way. Still, she sometimes hoped for something bigger than them all, but the opposite seemed to be true. It seemed there was no one there. She felt for her sandwich, opened it, and sunk her teeth in, finally quenching her long building hunger.

I have always worried about her becoming the type of person who was dependent on someone else. I believe that although Leona had us she always felt lonely and a little desperate because of the absence of her dad, even when my son lived with them. He was always a self-centered man. A thing like neglect can have long lasting consequences on a child regardless of how much the other people in a child's life try to make up for it. It's unfair, but true.

Anyway, I'm so proud of her, and I love Carlos, but I have a growing concern that Leona doesn't feel like she can do much without him. Hopefully this won't stop her from going to UCLA, if she gets in. I don't know what I'll do if she gets accepted and rejects the invitation. Let's think positive though. My sweet Leona is becoming quite the independent powerhouse, if I must say so myself.

As she stood on the bus holding on, she ate and thought of her life. Her oversized handbag with her books, laptop, and wallet was draped over her left shoulder, everything secured safely as she held on, swaying back and forth while eating and moving along towards the office. Sometimes she felt as if she was on a jungle boat floating down the river while monkeys hung on the trees and sea snakes sprung out of the water. Today was one of those days. She heard the sounds of toucans and something frog-like croaking outside the caravan, sounds echoing through the green canopy above. And then the lioness appeared, her round golden face peering through the brush as the humans tried and failed to find their way in this wilderness.

With this thought she couldn't help but smile at the thought of the jungle she had found herself in. Although it toppled her at times, it was quite an adventure.

The bus shook as it took a turn and she shifted her stance to regain balance. She would have grabbed onto the bar above her head, but couldn't reach it at an underwhelming 5'2, so she had to rely on a one-handed grip on the center pole. Feeling a bit lighter than earlier, she ate her sandwich, while trying to maintain balance. It was quite the task, but she was good at it.

A man across from her scowled, apparently thinking it was rude to be eating on the bus. She looked away, thinking he was rude for judging her.

In the midst of Leona's deep contemplation, the bus jolted forward like a rollercoaster and she lost her grip, causing her to fall to the ground. She lost her balance completely, flew forward, and found herself lying there with her belongings splayed all over the metal grating, her hands on the sticky metal surface. A few people gasped and leaned over to see if she was okay.

"You all right?" a woman who sat against the window a bit shaken herself, asked Leona.

"Um, yeah, I think so," she responded without knowing if

it was true. Sometimes you don't know how bad things are in the first moments of an accident. She looked around to make sense of it all. An elderly man who she'd seen earlier tried to help her pick her stuff up, but the bus was once again in motion, so he struggled to stand.

"It's okay, it's okay," Leona said, not wanting him to burden himself—or worse yet, fall like she had. She slowly got up and grabbed the center bar again as the bus had continued to move in its intended direction. The driver didn't even notice anything.

The elderly man leaned down and picked up some stray items despite her dismissal.

"Here you go, sweetie," he said as he handed her a spiral notebook that had spilled out of her bag. "I'm so sorry you fell."

Leona smiled up at him as she made her way off the ground. He had a certain goodness about him. "You better be careful. Looks like you're trying to do too much. Sometimes life has a way of slowing us down when we don't take initiative ourselves."

"Thank you," Leona said as she gathered the rest of her items and got onto a seat, trying to calm herself. "Yeah, I'm always doing too much."

"Don't you have anyone to help you out?" he asked in a slightly intrusive way that made her feel defensive for a moment. *Did he think she couldn't do it because she was a woman? Or maybe because she was young?* Both of these assumptions sat with her for a moment but then she brushed them away. "I'm doing fine. Thank you for your concern. I'll be okay," she said.

"Well, be careful, young lady. One day it might all catch up with you," he responded in the sort of way a loving grandfather would, and she could see that he cared. "You've got to look out for yourself."

"Well, I have a lot of people who love me, but thank you."

"I'm glad. So glad," he said and turned to look out the window.

The bus moved on and everyone went back to their private worlds of imagined tropical gardens, fast cars, and their very real world of cockroaches and long hours. Leona tried to go through her things to make sure nothing had gone missing, when she noticed that there was a large dark stain on her beige pant leg and a small rip on the elbow of her white button-up that was filling with blood. She pulled her shirt sleeve up to see a cut on her elbow and wondered how deep it was. Anger flooded her system, and she winced at the pain.

Fitting, she thought.

Suddenly, she remembered her sandwich and looked around. It was sitting on the dirty metal floor about six people over from her, next to someone's combat boots.

"Damn it," she grunted. She had only eaten one half of it.

A few people looked at her in pity and others seemed disgusted. As she moved to pick her sandwich up, she saw some other things on the ground, and then froze, paralyzed in sudden exhaustion. Although she'd stood up for herself earlier and had been feeling bigger, she still felt like an echo of someone mighty. It hit her like a punch and rage began to burn in her belly. She was tired of feeling angry. After a few minutes of staring out the window her angst turned to sulking. A rabbit caught her eye. It sitting on someone's lawn, as still as a stone.

Why do they do that? She thought. It had always seemed strange to her that they became statues when they smelled danger. *Maybe they were mourning their soon-to-be death? It's so counterintuitive.* She understood their paralysis as it seemed to replicate her life. She was frozen much of the time, and when she moved it was frantic, almost awkward.

As the bus moved forward, she noticed a blue and yellow

UCLA pen rolling around, almost as if it was tempting her to get it. The pen was from the day she'd gone to a workshop there and fallen in love with the program.

Everything is out of my grasp, she thought and turned away from the distraction.

The bus slowed, and she looked out to see Grand Park in front of her. Its green grass and the sun's shimmering haze lifted her spirits.

As the bus stopped, she looked back to thank the man who had helped her earlier, but saw he was reading *The Bluest Eye* by Toni Morrison. *No wonder,* she thought. It all made sense to her at that moment. The learners kept on getting smarter, and the struggling continued to fall; she wanted to be one of the learners. As she got off she reached down to grab her dirty sandwich and the pen.

It was then that I heard her speak to me. Her internal voice was small, almost tiny, but it's getting louder by the day.

Xochitl,

I'm exhausted. Why doesn't anything work? Can you tell me? I just lost everything on the bus, and I was in the middle of a sandwich–the first thing I'd eaten all day, mind you. I can't do this anymore.

Can you help me?

I'm going to make it eventually, I promise, but everything just seems so far out of reach right now. Will I survive? You did, I guess, so that gives me hope, but I do have my doubts. Whenever I feel down I think of you though and how you rose to so much out of so little. And... you did it with Dad and Aunt

Cecilia in tow. I can't believe that! I want to be like you, strong and confident. People think I am strong, but I'm not. I'm a puddle after the storm. One day, I want to be the rain. I don't want to hurt people, I don't. I'm just tired of being the recipient of the unexpected. I want to decide my days.

It's really Dad's fault. Sometimes I wonder if I did something to make him leave. Did I? He's the reason we have no money. If it weren't for him leaving, I'd probably be better off.

What she didn't know was that her dad's departure didn't have anything to do with her. He was high and making a habit of getting even higher when he ripped me off and left her and her mom. Drugs have their own agenda and while he was hurting them, his vice was swallowing him. When a person does something selfish out of addiction or self hate it's not connected to the victim but rather a reflection of the overpowering desire the addict has for their salve. This doesn't mean the action hurts the victim any less though, of course. That's for sure.

After he left them, he came to me. They don't have money because of my stupid mistake. I took out a loan from the equity on *my* house, and gave him the cash. I should have known he'd never paid it back. I lost my place in Silver Lake because of him. This house was what I planned to leave to Leona. This is why they're poor. Leona thinks I'm a perfect role model, and has never questioned me about any of it, but what she doesn't know is that I'm just as flawed as the rest of them. There is no perfect way to be.

She's much stronger than me in so many areas. I wish she knew this. Maybe she would stop beating herself up and have a little faith that she can do things. I mean, she's in school and everything...almost transferring, for goodness sake. I never did any of that. True, I did make it by becoming a singer and buying a place here in Los Angeles, that is something I am proud to have done, but she's strong in other ways. None of us went to college or had dreams of changing things. I was just trying to survive at her age. She actually wants to change the system. That's a great way to lead.

I wish I could send her something to give her energy and hope, but all I have is music.

Demented Doctor

I don't want to be brave; I want to be free.

* * *

For years, the infamous gymnastics team doctor, Larry Nassar, molested, harassed, and raped many of the gymnasts he worked with, including Rachael Denhollander (the first to come forward and accuse Nassar), Simone Biles (a eleven-time Olympic medalist), McKayla Maroney (two-time Olympic medalist), and Aly Raisman (six-time Olympic medalist). Over the course of the case investigating him, it was found that he had molested over 200 young women. There had been complaints throughout the years he coached but none were taken seriously.

When Denhollander came forward to file a Title IX complaint with Michigan State University and then shared her story of sexual abuse with the *Indianapolis Star*. Nassar sexually assaulted her numerous times when she was 15 years old under the pretense of helping her with her back pain. The university did not take the accusation seriously and allowed him to stay on staff and work with gymnasts while the investigation was under review.

Simone Biles, the 11-time Olympic champion, was one of the gymnasts Nassar sexually assaulted. In her statement before the Senate Judiciary Committee, she explained that the FBI didn't take action on the accusations in a timely manner and therefore Nassar was able to attack many other young women. She explained that this oversight, or rather negligence, caused tremendous harm to many young girls who should have been able to trust their coaches and the doctor they were sent to as part of the team.

Over the course of the trial, he was also found to have drugged and raped a young woman by the last name of Davis in 1992. She was given a pill by Nassar during an exam, when she was 17, and raped as a video camera captured the attack. When she became pregnant as a result of the attack, she notified MSU, but they did nothing.

They did not investigate him or turn him over to authorities and because of this he was able to go on for decades and continue to rape many other athletes. Eventually in 2017, Nassar was investigated and sentenced to serve a 40-170 year sentence, but not before he ravaged the lives of hundreds of aspiring athletes who trusted him to help them with their injuries.

12:15 p.m.

It happened so fast. They had just gotten back from lunch when the chaos hit them like a brick in the face. As Lucas opened the door to the warehouse, he watched a day laborer walk out of the enclosed room they'd been working in and yell something out before hitting the ground like a lazy noodle, slinking body, heavy head. The man was unconscious within seconds and everyone rushed up around him.

What happened? Did he get hit with something? What should we do? Are we in danger? All of these thoughts ran through Lucas' head as he stood there shocked. Scotty had gone back to headquarters, so it was up to him to figure things out.

After looking at him up close, it didn't seem that he was breathing. *That's the last thing I need*, he thought. "Call 911!" he yelled to Sergio. "He's out."

Sergio fumbled with his phone and dialed quickly. "Hello. Hello. We're on a job site and someone just passed out," he said. "Um...I don't know...hold on." He turned to Lucas who was hovering over the man and throwing water on him. "What's the address?"

"You don't know where we are....um...hold on," he said, realizing that he didn't know the address either. He searched his location. "608 Mateo," he yelled back. Tell them we're on the corner of 6th and Mateo in the old production building."

He tried to wake the worker, but he was not responding, so Lucas shook him harder until his head bobbed up and down against the concrete. The other workers looked on in dismay. They didn't seem to have any clue about what had happened.

"Wake up, Fucker," he mumbled under his breath.

It was then that Lucas realized he didn't even know the guy's name. He and Scotty had picked him up at a shop down the street to do the dirty work, but they never got his details. Lucas froze. This would get him in trouble, and the county might even shut the job down. Everyone knows you're not supposed to pick up day laborers without checking for their status. They all did it, but kept it quiet.

What if the guy is illegal? He probably is, Lucas thought.

"Shit," he yelled as the other workers watched. "What's in that room? Did you guys turn off the gas like I told you to?"

Everyone looked around, as Lucas yelled at them, trying to get information on what had happened.

"They don't understand," Sergio said.

"Well...fucking translate then," he yelled. "What if the gas is on? That means carbon monoxide might be pouring in."

12:28 p.m.

As Leona stepped off the bus she heard the birds chirping in the trees near the park and a light breeze met her face. She smiled for a moment and peace flooded her system.

Things will be okay, she thought.

A billboard across from her caught her attention as she gazed at the Los Angeles Apparel sign. There was a starved-looking woman in a 1980s style leotard bending over on it, a pained red look on her face. The objectification wafted into Leona's mind and brought the class discussion from earlier back. One of the articles she had read a few weeks ago was about the former Italian prime minister Berlusconi and how he had filled his cabinet with scantily dressed super models although they didn't have any political experience. The Italian population had risen up in angst against the sexual objectification and blatant misogyny. They marched with signs and yelled "basta." This story stuck with her because it shocked her–the fact that a president would do that. Also, one of her favorite words from childhood was posted on their signs. It seemed the desire to say "enough" was universal.

. . .

The street was bustling now and Leona made her way through the crowd. The law office she worked at was located up the street from Los Angeles City Hall, which she loved because of its art deco nod to the past, and its omniscient stature. She saw its wide white pillars sitting in the middle of dry stucco Cold War era box-like buildings and felt that they were like beautiful song birds in a junk yard. City Hall tapped into the romantic ideals that dwelled deep inside of her, and she suddenly felt good, nostalgia for an era that never truly existed. She wasn't ignorant enough to think things were actually better before though; everyone knew that things had only been better for men, and white ones at that. The architecture whispered to her–she liked that designers used to put more energy into making things gorgeous. It gave the average person hope–allowed them to dream amidst their daily life.

There was no time to daydream though. With this realization, she sped to the pace of a healthy jog and tried to focus on the task at hand. Her heavy bag slapped against her leg as she moved—a constant reminder of all she carried.

"Leoooonaaa!" Marcus sang as she stepped into the building. She had much more in common with the security guard than anyone upstairs, and the two of them reveled in their camaraderie. He had been there for a couple of years, like her, and he knew everyone and all of their business. She was always trying to get him to quit his job and go back to school because she saw a lot of potential in him, but he had a young daughter at home and no qualifications to do anything besides stand by the door and be a gatekeeper for those who were rising. He didn't have the luxury of being selective.

"What's up?" She smiled and met his fist with a bump. "I'm late again. You know what that means."

"Yeah, you're in for it. You look like you had a rough morning too," he said with a laugh as he glanced at the stain on her pants and the blood on her shirt. "God, what the hell happened to you? You get in a fight?"

"Pretty much...with the bus. The driver slammed on her brakes unexpectedly, causing me to kiss the floor, drop my bag, and lose my half eaten, but much desired, sandwich on the way down. I'm starving, and I look like shit," she said.

"No you don't," he said, shaking his head and checking to see how bad it was, "Well, maybe a little bit, but no one will notice." She doubted it was true, but it did make her feel better for a moment.

"Hopefully not. Is the bitch up there yet?" she asked, holding her breath for his answer. She hoped more than anything that Garcia wasn't in. Every once in a while her boss took a day off.

"Yeah, she came in about an hour ago," he said, making his eyes big. Like everyone else, Marcus knew that Garcia was a nightmare. People came out complaining about her all the time, and he had heard the worst of it because they were usually most upset after a long day with her. "Better go before she comes down here looking for you!"

"Yeah, you're lucky you're not up there. It's much safer here." She grinned at him. "Maybe she won't notice I'm late."

"I somehow doubt that," he said, eyebrows raised.

Leona sighed a long exhale and entered the elevator. It ascended swiftly, and before she could get her story together, she was out, heading down the hall to the jungle that was the law firm. The hallway wound on for a while, twisting and turning like a wild river. She passed a doctor's office that specialized in Parkinson's and a therapist's suite where people often came out crying. She wondered whether patients were just paying money to sob. It seemed so depressing. This was part of the reason she refused therapy; she didn't need any more tears.

"God, Leona. What is it this time? You're a mess," Garcia barked immediately as she entered the office to her misfortune. Her boss happened to be standing right near the door, talking to one of the three administrative assistants when she walked in.

Leona met eyes with Garcia's wolf-like gaze.

"You don't seem to understand," Garcia continued, glaring at her while others in the room turned to see the latest circus. "Do you know how many people want your job?"

Leona's blood began to boil. It seemed as if her tipping point had arrived.

Be calm. Blowing up won't change anything, she thought. *Don't get fired.*

Garcia continued, "And why do you look like a goddamn train wreck?"

"Um... I..." she stammered, fighting with her thoughts. *How much should I say?* It took all of her power to hold back. Her ability to contain herself seemed to have shrunk dramatically throughout the day, but saying anything was dangerous for her prospects with the law firm. She looked at Garcia and thought of all of the things she wished to say. Her boss was used to speaking however she saw fit and she treated everyone as if they were insignificant. She breathed in deeply and thought of becoming water.

I had always told her that was the way to be.

Flow around the chaos, Leona thought. *Be like water.* She looked Garcia in the eye.

"I..." she began.

"What? You what? What's your excuse this time?" Garcia interrupted, seemingly unaware or apathetic of the inner tug a war Leona was experiencing.

"I fell on the bus," she finally spit out. "It slammed on its breaks, and I flew forward. I feel horrible."

"You fell?" Garcia asked, looking at her up and down, trying to decide if she bought the explanation. Then she huffed and paused, seemingly deciding whether to let Leona go or to tear into her more. After a moment, she exhaled and said, "Alright, then. Get to work. Take this seriously, damn it, or you won't be here much longer."

Leona nodded as a servant would while screaming obscenities in her head, as she made her way to the back where her cubicle was. Her coworkers looked up at her, some nodding to say hello.

How cruel. How unsupportive, Leona thought as she hustled. *One day I'll be the boss, and I won't talk to people like that.* Her bones ached for retribution, but she also felt alone, unseen. *Didn't Garcia know she was trying her best? Wasn't it obvious?*

And one day I will tell her off, she thought. *Hopefully it will be sooner rather than later.* Her chest burned with the thought and she allowed herself to run wild in the idea for a moment, imagining everything she would say.

Maybe she wasn't such a pacifist.

* * *

The requests had already lined up for the day, and her inbox was stacked. One tap was all it took to cause a traffic jam. There was so much to do and none of it had much meaning to her. She was only there for the possible future it might secure.

Leona, did you remember the candles? A message from Lucinda, the office manager, read.

Shit, she thought. It had been the furthest thing from her mind, but it was the one thing they asked her to do for Garcia's birthday celebration that was planned for later that day.

Her gaze rested on the message. First she felt disappointed but then apathy set in. *So what*, she thought as she read it over again. *Garcia is such a horrible person. She doesn't deserve a party.*

"Morning," Freddie, her best friend at work, said, interrupting her thoughts. His "scurry like a mouse" mannerisms mixed with Latin pop singer looks gave him quite the confusing image. People always thought he was attractive until they heard his voice.

"It's not morning," she said.

"Sour mood?" he questioned, looking down at her and then continued. "I just heard Garcia. She was ranting about you before you got here...said something about how this was the last time."

"Oh God, great," Leona shot back. "She doesn't even know I forgot the candles yet."

"Uh oh, you're in for it," Freddie said in a sigh. "You'd better tell Lucinda before we get too close to party time. Maybe she'll have time to run out and do your job."

"Don't rub it in. You know I already feel like shit. And you're not any better. You never have to do anything."

"True," he admitted. He was always given the tasks no one cared about.

"And why does Lucinda even have me getting stuff for her anyways. I don't have a car. I'm not the fucking office manager. They should have had someone else do it. Like you.

Why don't you ever have to do anything? They always leave it to us, like all women love party planning or something. So sexist. I hate parties."

In this moment she remembered how I'd told her about how female workers used to be required to serve men coffee when in a meeting, even if they had similar positions. They were limited to hostess-type activities whenever service was required. In this thought, Leona noticed that not much had changed and scoffed at the lack of progress. Women were still doing all of the housekeeping everywhere.

"Yeah, I'm not complaining," he said and laughed. "All I have to do is eat. By the way, I heard we're having tacos," he said as he licked his lips and tried to take the attention off of himself. "They probably know we'd do a bad job, Leo. That's why no one ever asks us to do anything."

"I'd do a bad job, actually. I've proven it. See...," she pointed down at an empty desk and laughed. "No candles."

Behind Freddie, Leona saw Garcia begin to walk towards them and then sighed when she turned into the conference room instead. "God Dammit. She makes me so nervous."

"She's pure evil. It doesn't matter what you do; she'll always find something wrong." Freddie said as he leaned in closer to Leona so no one could hear. "I heard she's getting a divorce."

"You're such a chismoso," Leona giggled and then continued. "That's not surprising. I wonder if she treats her husband that way?" Leona tried to imagine being married to someone who barked and criticized. Her dad had been that way, before he left, and she always wondered why her mom put up with it. Leona knew she'd never lie down like that for any partner, and although Carlos was a gentle soul, she promised herself she would be brave and swift if he ever shifted to darkness.

"Probably," Freddie said, pondering Garcia's homelife. "Can you imagine how bad it must be if he messes up at all? Poor guy."

"If I ever meet him, I'll take him out to celebrate his escape. Hurray for getting out. Hurray for leaving the beast." Freddie laughed.

"I better get back to it," Freddie said. "I'll catch up with you later."

I forgot the candles, Leona texted Lucinda, hoping to receive an understanding message. Women supporting women, right?

Wtf, Leona. I seriously asked you for one thing. Urg...

Leona grimaced at the response.

Sorry, no car. You know that. And I have school before this. Sad Face emoji. That was the best she could do.

Fine. whatever. See if I ask you for help again. Lucinda responded quickly. *I guess I'll have to do it myself.*

For a moment Leona felt deflated as it seemed she could never do anything right but then she switched back to anger. *Good,* she thought. *Please don't ask me for anything. I have enough to do.*

But instead of texting this, she responded: *so sorry. Bad day.*

Lucinda wrote back without a second's pause. *We all have them.*

Leona couldn't tell if the message was sympathetic or spiteful, but she decided to let it go and assume the former. There was no use for contemplation.

As she got deep into her work, her mind began to wander and her guilt subsided. She looked outside the office window to see a tall palm tree waving its fingers at her and beckoning her.

That's where she wanted to be. Despite her stress, she closed her eyes for a moment and imagined the escape. Maybe she was on an island. Maybe if she walked outside right now, the hot black streets would fade away and melt into an aqua blue ocean water that came up to kiss her toes. Maybe there were sea turtles eating from the sea's grass and weaving in and out of the rocks. The air conditioning above her head was an onshore tropical breeze from the ocean. She could lightly hear Bad Bunny in the background at someone's desk and this swept her further into her imaginary world. This led her into thoughts of her past, where she had once been a child who was mesmerized by the earth.

Back then, she built tiny dams on the side of the road with the miniature stones she had picked up from the neighborhood park. She spent hours analyzing the shades and shapes of the treasures she dug out of the ground. There was so much it had to offer; the beauty and power of the natural world held her full attention. In Silver Lake, she had always focused on the tiny bits of nature embedded in her environment. That little child was still sitting inside of her waiting to play and she sometimes felt her creep up and ask for some attention. We all have this former self inside, but some of us have pushed the existence so far down we don't know how to find them.

Back when she was very young and happy, before moving to San Juan Capistrano for most of her elementary years, she lived in my old house in Los Angeles, near Silver Lake Meadows where there were trails, trees, and plenty of insects and animals. There were no longer many animals there, as the people had taken over much of the land and made it inhospitable for them, but in the past it was quite full of wildlife.

Leona always seemed most at home in wild spaces. I'm the same; I guess maybe we all are?

Leona's phone buzzed on her desk, interrupting her thoughts. It was a voice message from her mom. She picked it up and listened, thinking it might be important. The chances were slim, but there was always a possibility. She'd have something valuable to say.

Hi Honey, did you hear about all of the protests? I'm wondering why people are so upset about this guy? Seems like he'd do our country well. I like how he speaks his mind. It's about time for that and of course the deep state is so mad about what he said about Mexicans. It's true sometimes though. It's true.

The candidate she was referring to had just smothered immigrants with all kinds of disgusting slander and Leona's liberal heart beat fiercely as she remembered what had been said in his speech the night before. *What a racist,* she thought, *and the deep state? What did her mom know? She was entirely uneducated.* It was infuriating. She knew her mom wasn't racist, but it was difficult to understand how uninformed she was. She tried to finish listening to the message calmly but ended up cringing the entire time.

I think he'd be good for us, she continued. *I mean, look at how bad things are. He's not a politician. That's what we need right now. It's refresh....*

Leona dropped the phone from her ear and deleted the message. She couldn't stomach the stupidity. The sadness about her mom devoured her as she fell into a long dark underground tunnel that sucked her feet in and collapsed her lungs into vertical pancakes. *I think he'd be good for us.* She could hear her mom saying. The phrase echoed in the chambers of her mind until they dissolved.

She quickly texted her mom back: *They are protesting*

because he shouldn't be saying stupid racist things like that or even thinking that way. Mexicans aren't rapists, Mom. Why are you okay with this? It's disgusting. Carlos is Mexican. Is he a rapist? And what about Xavier, huh? Is he? Dad is part Mexican too. I know you're upset with him, but he's not a criminal. I'm busy, Mom. Love you. Let me know if you really need anything. If not, see you tonight and stop watching TV. It's poisoning your mind.

Out of the corner of her eye, Leona saw Garcia lumbering towards her and she thought, *Shit, the meeting must be over and I'm obviously distracted.* Chairs shuffled around her and everyone looked more intently at their computers as Garcia walked over. The talk in the office had been talking about a sexual assault case that Garcia had been working on; it wasn't going as planned, and as a result, she had an even shorter fuse than normal. The case was an important one; she was prosecuting an assailant who had viciously attacked a 23-year-old Thai woman on her way home from work last year. The man yelled something out to her and when she turned around to see what the commotion was, he ran up to her, spit in her face, yelled "go back to China." Then, according to a witness, he drug her into an alleyway and raped her in broad daylight. He was halfway through his destruction when someone ran up and yelled for him to stop. He took off running, leaving her there half naked and helpless. The victim was a young mother on her way home from the market she worked at with grocery bags full of fruit and sandwich meat for her kids. Every time Leona thought about the case, her world began to spin.

As she stood there watching Garcia rush around the office, she felt a slight tilt of being off balance (the mere thought of rape shook her), but nothing like she had experienced earlier that day. Within all of Garcia's faults, there was one glowing attribute: she fought hard to get justice for her clients. Leona tried to focus on this. Garcia was hungry for a win and that was a good thing. Leona knew that even if she won, however, her client would never be vindicated. No amount of money could undo the terror. The innocent mother would have to live with the crime that was committed against her body and mind for the rest of her life.

Asian Fetish

I don't want to be brave; I want to be free.

* * *

In March of 2021, a gunman rushed into multiple massage parlors, killing nine people, six who were Asian, and injuring eight others. He stated that he had to do it because the massage parlors were tempting him to do things "that he shouldn't be doing" and he blamed a sexual addiction.

The 21 year old had planned to commit suicide later that night, and as he sat outside of the massage parlor contemplating whether paying for sex would motivate him to do so, he decided to shoot them instead.

The objectification of Asian women has led to harassment and assault in many different instances. Being that international military bases are adjacent to the sex worker industries in many Asian countries, the idea of an Asian fetish has grown.

Destructive stereotypes hold that Asian women are

submissive and hyper sexual which makes them targets. During the pandemic of 2020 these stereotypes converged with a growing hate for Asians due to the scapegoating politicians, beginning with Trump, used to blame for the transmission of the Covid 19 virus. There was a dramatic increase in hate crimes against Asians, mostly women, and a subsequent increase in sexual crimes against the same group.

2:19 p.m.

Garcia hustled past Leona's desk without glancing her way and she was happy to be invisible for once. She contemplated Garcia's supposed divorce and it made her think of her own father's disappearance. After an especially long disagreement between her parents, when she was 12 years old, she woke up to her father's absence. She had known intuitively that her days with him were numbered, as she could feel them escaping like steam through an open bathroom door, but she didn't expect him to disappear completely.

Freddie turned the corner and walked towards her, his man bun flopping around on the top of his head. He had just gotten out of a meeting with Garcia and looked tired. "What a bitch. It wasn't just you. She's in a ripe mood today." He smiled a toothy grin. "Hope that makes you feel better."

"It does actually," she said.

An intern across the way wore a UCLA shirt, reminding her to check her email. "I better check to see if I got into UCLA."

"Are decisions coming out today?"

"They've been rolling out for days, but I haven't heard anything yet."

"You'll get in, and if so, I want to be the first to congratulate you," he said.

She looked down at her phone, suddenly protective. She didn't want him to be the first one to know. That is, *if* she got in. To her, the chances were slim. Imposter syndrome was hard fastened in her psyche.

There was nothing important in her inbox, however, as she stared at emails for retail stores.

"Nothing," she said as Freddie waited in anticipation.

He looked at her in disappointment. "I'm sure it will come soon, and you'll get in. You're smart."

She turned to Freddie and smiled gratefully. "You know we'll be out of this one day, right?"

"Out of what?" he asked.

"This place, this hellhole, where we have to wait on people and let them treat us like trash."

"Woah, It's not that bad," he said. "You okay?"

"Yeah, this just bugs me—the fact that we're here in these lowly positions and have been for so long without much movement. I think I'm just tired of being a "yes man" all of the time. I don't want to be the underdog any longer," she paused assessing their surroundings. "You've got to get back to school too. Do it, Freddie. Why are you waiting? You have less time than you know."

"I think I have a lot of time. Honestly, I have nothing but time, but I'll think about it."

"Don't 'think about it' do it. We've got to stay focused and get it done. Remember, people like us don't graduate. You know that, right?" she asked.

He nodded in agreement, thinking about all of his friends who dropped out of college and were stuck in retail jobs.

"Remember the friend I told you about who got that great marketing position for the Dodgers?" Leona continued. "Well, she was in the right spot at the right time and she had the degree so she qualified for the job. If she hadn't pushed through though, it wouldn't have been an option for her."

"I know, you always talk about her."

"She's one of the few people I know who put her head down and finished. She was fully in, so when she submitted her name for the job, and the HR team at the company she had interned with spoke to people who knew her, it did the trick. It's all about being prepared and knowing people."

"Okay, okay...I hear you," he said. "You're starting to sound like my mom."

She continued, ignoring him. "Think about it, most people in our shoes don't do well or know anyone who is doing well, let alone someone who is thriving. That's why it's so hard for us to get ahead. But *we* know people because of this shitty job. Look around. They may be assholes but they are probably our best tie to the next level."

He looked around and nodded. "You're right but you're also really bossy. I'll do it."

"I'm not bossy, I'm just a woman who knows what she wants," she retorted.

"Yes, you are, but it's annoying," he said.

Her face dropped because she suddenly felt hurt by his brashness. She was tired of being called bossy.

Freddy seemed to notice. "Leona, if anyone is going to make it, it will be you."

"Thanks," she said. "Yes, I will fucking make it and so will you. Now get back to school."

. . .

A door opened, and Garcia began to make her way down the hallway again, coming at them. Leona brushed him away and looked at her computer.

"I better get going," Freddie said. "This is a weird day. Garcia is unpredictable. Maybe because it's her birthday?"

"Oh yeah, I forgot."

"Yes, you did."

"Shut up."

2:49 p.m.

"He's down at LA General," Lucas said to Scotty over the phone after the warehouse had emptied and the worker had been taken to the hospital. No one knew the man's name, so Lucas just sent him anonymously. Hopefully he'd wake up. Hopefully someone would get him to his family. Hopefully things would work out. Lucas considered all of this and felt a tinge of guilt for not doing his job right, but he was mostly worried about liability. He knew he had to notify Scotty.

"What happened? Did you check everything out before the guys started working?" his boss pried, as he tried to explain it to him.

"Yes, of course," he lied. Dishonesty was no new task for him as he'd grown up covering his tracks and trying to avoid the wrath of The General. Nothing helps someone perfect lying like growing up in an abusive household. "I'm not sure what happened. I walked in after we got back from lunch and he was lying there on the ground."

"Sounds like it might be a gas leak. You know to always

double check that stuff, right?' He paused and cleared his throat.

"Yes, of course," Lucas answered. "I'm not an idiot."

"What the fuck could it be?" Lucas had never heard Scotty acknowledge stress before. It shook him, and he realized that both of them would get in trouble, possibly even fired, if the worker didn't wake up. "Let's just hope he's okay," Scotty continued with a keen look in his eyes. "For your sake, you better hope he is."

"Are you going to mention it to Joe?" Lucas asked as he backed up. If his boss found out about the oversight he was sure to be fired. "Everything will work out. No need to worry him."

He waited for a response as he surveyed the job site. Everything was all over the place, and he thought about how he'd turned the gas off shortly after the medics had left. Only he knew. He wondered if anyone else was sick.

"What if it's something serious though? We can't have guys passing out all over the place," Scotty asked.

"I sent them home," Lucas responded. "I know we have a lot to do, but I was nervous that more guys would get sick. It's just me and Sergio here now, but I think we can get it done."

"Okay, that's good," Scotty replied. "I guess I'll hold off telling Joe."

"Maybe the guy was just starving or something. I didn't see him take a break with everyone else, but then again we were gone. Maybe he's diabetic?." he elaborated, trying to placate Scotty. "Honestly, I think it's a good idea to stay quiet about this. If Joe finds out, we may have to shut the job down and then we'll lose so much time, and they'll lose money. Some things are better left unsaid. Don't you think?"

"True, true" Scotty replied as he considered his options. "Well, it's a risk not to say anything, but maybe you're right."

"You know..." Lucas began and then paused, "we could

deny ever picking him up. We could say he was a homeless person who wandered in. No one knew his name or anything."

Scotty stopped to think. "Hmm...that's a solid idea.'

"I mean everyone is gone besides Sergio, and I think I could get him to keep quiet," Lucas finished. He'd sent Sergio outside so that he could survey the situation alone after the worker had been taken by the paramedics. He hoped to find the origin of the problem in solitude. He was glad he'd thought of sending Sergio outside before noticing the gas was on. "Serg is a good guy, and he's pretty desperate for work. I think he'll comply."

"Okay then, let's stick with that story. We don't know the guy...he must have wandered in while we were out getting food," Scotty began. "As long as no one else shows up, we're in the clear."

"Sounds good."

"Wait, what did you tell the medics?"

"Honestly nothing. I just said I walked in and he was lying there," Lucas answered. "They were in such a hurry they didn't ask many questions. I just explained what happened loosely. Luckily I had gotten out before then.

Sergio walked in and Lucas nodded to acknowledge him, getting off of the phone with Scotty. "Okay, gotta go. Sergio is here and we have a lot of work to do. Got to make up for lost time. Talk soon."

"Alright, I will pop over again later. Make sure you get out if you notice anything weird. We don't need more accidents."

Sergio looked over at Lucas. "We're gonna keep working?" he asked.

"Yeah, it's all good. No worries," Lucas said quickly. "Let's get to it."

3:12 p.m.

Leona's constant hunger reminded her of her belly's hollow state. She fumbled around her desk for the cash she thought she'd left there: $1.76 was all she could find. It would have to hold her over until she got to work at McDonald's later that evening. Shift leaders got a free meal.

The growl in her stomach pushed her to the vending machine, and she quickly purchased some cashews, thinking it might hold her over.

Some women don't eat on purpose, she thought as she scarfed down the nuts, thankful for the nuts. It had always shocked her that some people purposely starved themselves as she had and her family had to hunt around for food. She understood why–societal pressure to be thin and all of that–but it still struck her as unbearable. Nothing was worth the empty feeling of hunger.

When she got back to her desk, a painting of the zocalo in Guadalajara across the way at her coworker's desk caught her eye and reminded her to ask Jas to make a call about Xavier when she got home. She missed him. Thoughts of her stepdad filled her mind. He was the closest thing she'd known to a dad and she couldn't believe he was gone. He was one of her biggest supporters and she often thought about what a good person he was. His heart bled equality and he helped her to believe in herself and her value as well. She loved him and his feminist spirit.

She thought about the men in her life and their connection to Mexico. Both Xavier and Carlos were from small towns outside of Guadalajara and because of the association with two people she loved so fiercely she had developed an affinity for the city, although she'd never been there. In the painting a bright yellow cathedral-looking building stood tall with the blue sky behind it. Leona loved to look at it not just because of the contrasting colors, but also because she hoped to visit one day after she and Carlos decided to marry. With this thought a thousand swallows descended onto her desk and lifted her into the air by her shirt tails, suspending her feet off of the ground for a brief interlude and twirling her around while happily singing a story of love. Everyone she knew would be there and it would be a day devoted to bold dreams and eternal love. She beamed in this thought as sunlight streamed through the windows and the green palms waved their fronds at her in celebration.

But Carlos didn't have his papers and their wallets were empty, so the ideas of birds and dreams slipped away. This didn't make her want it any less. Maybe they could escape to Mexico, and while they were at it, find Xavier over there too. Her mind was suddenly filled with hope: *Maybe he was back in his hometown right outside of the city and unable to reach out for some reason. Or maybe he was too mad at her mom to do so? But no, he'd never leave his son or her and keep quiet. She had to figure out where he was.*

Before Jas moved in with them, and after she'd already moved to LA she spent a good amount of time with Xavier.

Her step brother had been with his mom at that time, and she didn't allow him time with Xavier, so he poured all of his fatherly love into Leona. She felt like she had a dad again. She grew to love him tenderly and the hunger for a father subsided for a while. Xavier was a quality man. He taught her everything that her own father hadn't. Where hers had been impatient, Xavier was lavishly unrushed. Whereas her dad was flush with anxiety, Xavier was filled with calm. Even now, when she was stressed, Xavier was one of the people who came to mind. Even in his absence he helped her.

Family creates a person and the collection of the people involved in the circle make up the tapestry of what those bones hold. The bond begins to form in childhood and solidifies into the teen years and then the experiences seep out like slowly dripping honey as the years go by.

As she fact-checked legal documents she remembered how Xavier affected her. One day came to mind. He had been patiently showing her how to make bread from scratch right after they moved to L.A. Each step was part of a predictable pattern. It was easy as long as you followed the clear directions, and it had a cathartic feeling to it. Hands on. Mind free.

* * *

"You add three times as much flour as you do water," Xavier had explained slowly, waiting for her to acknowledge her understanding. "Just remember, one-half a cup of starter, a full cup of room temperature water, and then three cups of flour. That feeds it."

"It feeds it? Yes, every living thing needs food and sourdough is alive."

"Okay. Now what?" Leona asked eagerly. She had been so

curious at the age of thirteen and was everything but patient. "Do I get my hands in there?"

"Yes, move it around first until it's one big ball, then knead it with your knuckles to get any little flour knots out. It's just like life; you have to massage it until it works for you," he explained. "Once all of the flour is incorporated, you're done. Take your time."

Leona remembered twisting the dough in a clockwise motion, careful not to let the flour spill out of the bowl, and then pressing down on the gooey substance to help it fully attach to itself. It stuck to her fingers like mud and was quite uncomfortable.

"See how it's sticky? That means you have to add more flour in order to get the right consistency," he explained. "Everything is about balance. You have to find what works by experimenting."

Xavier fed a part of her that wanted to grow.

* * *

"You really set Lucinda off," Freddie said as he stood in front of her for the second time that day. She was deep in thought and barely looked up as he approached. Living in the world of bread making was a much nicer place to be.

"Well, whatever. She shouldn't have asked me. It's her job. She gets paid to do all of that stuff." Behind them, Leona saw Lucinda rushing out the front door. Leona's stomach dropped for a moment.

"You're in a ripe mood," he said scoffing.

She looked up at him, sitting in his wide gaze for a moment, and then suddenly fell into a hole as the ground swallowed her.

"I'm just done, Freddie," she said. "I'm so tired and this

day has destroyed me. I'm having a hard time caring about birthday parties and candles, sorry."

He softened, putting on his listening face.

"Spill it," he said. Freddie always loved drama, and she knew this, but also appreciated the fact that he would listen.

"There's not enough time," she said. "Plus, the party will start soon, and I have so much work to do."

"Well, just give me the shortened version then."

"Okay," she said, clearing her throat. "I was groped by some unhoused pervert at the bus stop, then I got into a huge fight in class with some self-hating woman, I fell on the bus, dropped everything all over the disgusting floor, and got hurt in the process, then I got here late and was yelled at, and now I'm sitting here feeling bad about forgetting stupid candles for the woman who spat hate at me when I entered. Truth is, all I want to do is climb into my bed and sleep for a very long time, but if I do so everything will just crumble."

"Ouch, that's a lot." he lowered his eyes and studied some scratches that were on the counter. "So sorry."

"You think?" she said in jest. "I'm just waiting to see how things get worse. I still have McDonalds tonight and something always goes down there. I swear, we never have a peaceful night."

"You'll be fine," he said, trying to console her for a moment, "sounds like all of the bad stuff has already happened." After a minute, he got a mischievous look in his eyes and asked, "So what was the fight about? Was it good? I love a good girl fight."

"Weirdo," she said, laughing at his comment and then tried to decide whether to divulge the information. "It was good. I did 'win' if you want to know...but I embarrassed myself in the process. I really blew up, and I called her stupid."

"Ooh, sounds fun..."

"Well, this chick actually had the audacity to say that rape isn't that big of an issue and that talking about it is making things worse. Can you believe that?"

He leaned harder into the counter, thinking for a moment. "Well, I don't know."

"What do you mean you 'don't know'?" she said as anger turned in her belly.

Freddie glanced behind him, making sure Garcia was nowhere to be found and then continued. "Of course, rape is horrible, but I'm not sure talking about it helps."

"Oh god, are you fucking kidding me?" She asked wide eyed in an obviously angry whispered yell. "You sound just like her. I'm just so tired of this," she said as she threw her hands down onto her keyboard and looked away from him.

"Whoa, whoa," he said as his eyes widened and he leaned in more, trying to keep things quiet. "I was about to say that I don't know how much it helps to talk about it because we really need to teach men to be better and we need more accountability, better laws, and stuff. Not that it doesn't matter. You know I'm not like that."

Looking up in embarrassment, she said,"Oh sorry, I'm just exhausted. I should have known you weren't saying that."

"Yeah, you should have. What's wrong with you today?" Freddie asked as he stepped back a bit.

"Fuck, I don't know..." Leona said.

In this moment, Leona reminded me of myself at her age. Back in the 70's it was common for men, and even women for that matter, to think that it was best to brush the sexual assault under the rug and pretend that nothing happened. Because of this, I remember assuming that everyone was of that mindset and even when they tried to agree with me, I would naturally assume that they were against me. It's hard being a vocal woman in a world that wants us quiet..

I remember people pushing rape away as part of sexuality and saying things like "boys will be boys" and "she'd dress differently if she knew what was good for her" or sometimes even claiming they liked aggressive men or saying that dominance was "hot." Statements like that were common, and it really made us frustrated when we tried to discuss the real issue. After reading one of Audrey Lorde's speeches in the 80's where she said, "rape is not aggressive sexuality, it is sexualized aggression," the conversation was forever changed for me, and I later wrote about it to the girls in my family.

Poor Freddie, he seems like a sweet man. Little did he know his friend was at her end.

Leona answered her last email in haste and logged off. She could see Garcia in the conference room acting surprised at the swanky charcuterie board and fuchsia colored cake that sat before her. She assumed the party had started and knew she better get in there before Garcia took it personally. Everyone was gathered around her, but they were still keeping their distance, feigning excitement. 'Happy Birthday!' She could hear from across the hall. Thoughts of quickly ditching the office ran across her mind, but her feet walked towards the party and her lips said, "Happy Birthday!" as she leaned in for an obligatory hug with the giant bully.

Freddie stood across from Leona, still uncomfortable from earlier. He met eyes with her, but looked away. He didn't deserve the brashness she'd served him, and she knew it. After a moment of contemplation, she looked back and mouthed sorry again.

He feigned anger for a moment and then smiled. She never felt more grateful for his friendship than in that moment. He was one of the good ones.

. . .

In the late afternoon light, surrounded by coworkers and their stories, Garcia didn't seem as daunting, and for a moment, she even looked like a normal person. She was, after all, fighting to help women go against their perpetrators. With this in mind, Leona thought she caught a glimpse of softness in Garcia while she was talking to Lucinda and she hoped she was right. Suddenly she had the horrifying realization that she could become just as rude and cynical as Garcia in a few years if she wasn't careful. She was developing the same tough skin and it was the opposite of what she wanted for herself.

Morality Police

I don't want to be brave; I want to be free.

* * *

Mahsa Amini was taken to a reeducation class in Iran in 2022 after refusing to wear her headscarf. She was only 22 years old at the time and was part of a larger group of women who were fighting back against the strict rules regarding women's dress in Iran at the time.

After 26 minutes in detention with the Morality Police, Amini collapsed and was later taken to a hospital where she died. The coroner said that she died from the overwhelmingly brutal assault on her body: both physically and sexually.

News of her death sparked protests all over the country and women took off their head scarves as a form of rebellion for both her death and for the limiting laws regarding women's dress. Over the course of the protests, more than 500 protestors were killed by the morality police and many of the women who were out on the streets were shot in the eye intentionally to mark them as outsiders.

Additionally, a huge number of women have been raped and beaten while in the custody of the morality police since Amini's death. This catastrophe has sparked outrage and protests all over the world but it has not changed policy.

3:15 p.m.

Sergio went to the back room where the man had been working before he fell and looked around at the shelving unit and left over tools and appliances. He noticed the gas gauge and realized in that moment that he had been right about his suspicions. *Lucas is such an asshole*, he thought. He didn't recall seeing Lucas go back to switch it off or tell anyone else to do so before they had gotten started. He bent down to make sure it was in the off position and sighed.

That poor guy, he thought, feeling for the innocent worker, and wondering how someone like Lucas had been promoted to being a foreman while *he* was still scrounging for work like a beginner. *I never would have let this happen.*

"Serg," Lucas howled from the main room. "Can you help me lift this motherfucker and take it out to the truck?"

Sergio sighed and then pivoted, catching a glimpse of himself in the mirror for just a moment and seeing himself a little too clearly. His hair was turning gray prematurely. He played with it for a moment, tossing it this way and that. He was only thirty, but he looked to be in his forties. Maybe it was the rugged life he'd lived and all of the turmoil his family had gone through. Maybe it was genetics.

"Coming..." he said as he put his thoughts away and made his way out to meet Lucas. As he stepped out of the room his phone buzzed. It was his wife. He had called earlier, but she hadn't answered because they were busy now that the other guys had been let go. He ignored it again and moved toward Lucas who was picking up the end of an old tool box. It was good enough to keep. They knew that if they left it, the box would be demolished along with the walls around them. Sergio hoisted the metal frame up onto a dolly and maneuvered it out the front door so they could lift it into the truck.

"This will be awesome in my garage," Lucas said, as he shoved it in the bed. "I've been wanting something better to put all of my junk in."

Sergio looked at him through the blazing sun.

"I'm going to step out for a minute and take a cigarette break," Sergio said, needing a break from Lucas. He wanted to call his wife and tell her about the gas leak and the guy who had passed out but he knew he should stay quiet.

Lucas nodded in agreement. "No worries, but be fast. We have a ton to do."

Yeah, because you are a fucking idiot and didn't do your job. Sergio thought. He remained silent though. There were more important things at hand.

"Hi sweetheart," Sergio said as she answered. "How are the girls?" He wanted nothing more than to be at home with them at the moment, playing with his kids, in the company of better people.

"Oh, they are wearing me out," Celene answered. "When are you getting home? I saw you called earlier but Jenny was wrapped up in the dog's leash and I had to spend a good fifteen minutes untangling her. She's such a silly girl. I guess she was walking Pepe and he started doing circles around her. Before she knew it, she was all wrapped up in his leash and couldn't get out. She came crying over to me, dog in tow."

He laughed. "She's a goofball. Did you take a picture?"

"Yeah, I'll send it," she said. "What's up though? Why did you call?"

Sergio took a breath, knowing Celene would tell him to come home if he let her know what had happened. She would say nothing was worth the money, that he shouldn't put himself in danger, and other logical things like that. He could hear a giggle in the background and he imagined his house with the silly bundles of children filling the walls. It warmed him.

"Some guy, a worker Lucas picked up, passed out about an hour ago, and he's in the hospital," he said. "I think he's fine, but I'm guessing they forgot to turn the gas off. It's so irresponsible. I hope the guy doesn't have brain damage or anything. Of course Lucas isn't admitting anything. He's acting like nothing happened."

"What? Get out of there. That's insane. What if there is something else going on? What if it's toxic in some way? I love you. I think you should leave," she said. "It's not worth it."

He smiled, feeling loved, but then realized he wasn't going to do what she wanted. They couldn't afford it. "Nah, it's all fine now. I promise I'll be careful."

"Baby, please. Don't risk it," she said.

Lucas stepped around the corner, eyeing him, and pointing at his imaginary watch.

"Got to go, sweetie. I'll see you soon, I promise," he said. "Don't worry."

. . .

As he hung up and walked back towards Lucas he tried to act calm although his mind was racing. *What if she is right?,* he thought.

"Cigarette break, huh? I didn't think you smoked," Lucas said in a laugh. "What did your wife say? She wants you to leave?"

Sergio looked up to meet his eyes. "What? Nah, she was just telling me about the girls.. We're all good. Let's get back to work." He had hoped Lucas didn't notice he was on the phone with her.

"You're pussy whipped," Lucas shot back. "Okay, let's get back inside. This place isn't going to empty itself.

"At least I have someone to go home to," Sergio answered. He couldn't let the slight go. Although he knew Lucas' contempt came from jealousy it irked him. Sergio only knew a little bit about Lucas' history with women but he knew enough to come to a conclusion.

Before Lucas' last girlfriend left him, she said three words: I hate you. These words echoed in his mind for months after she shut the door to his apartment and disappeared.

The feeling is mutual, he had thought at the time.

She had been a pain to be with, always wanting to hang out, asking him to ditch his friends, expecting him to play less video games, and she had the most unattractive laugh he'd ever heard. He just couldn't stand it. Plus, she was weak. She never stood up for herself no matter what he did. She just took the pummeling.

One night stood out in his memory as holding its own whenever he thought about Madison.

They'd gone to a party at their friend Susana's downtown bungalow, and it was running later than usual. Lucas was tired, and looking for Madison so they could go home, when he heard what he thought was a laugh. It ended up being a whimper. He went downstairs into the alley to find Madison wrapped up in an embrace with her old boyfriend and crying. Before he could even question her intentions or ask what had happened, he found himself on top of the man. In an instant, his fists crashed into the boyfriend's face crushing his nose and pulverizing his cheekbones. He didn't know who he'd become and in the heat of everything Lucas flashed back to his childhood violence. He could hear The General yelling. Sweat poured down his neck as he dove in further, but then his little brother Tyler's face crept into focus which slowly caused him to relent. He couldn't do this. Not again.

Without saying anything, he got up and walked away leaving Madison crying and her ex boyfriend bleeding on the sidewalk.

She never forgave him for attacking her ex-boyfriend. According to her, he had been consoling her about her friend's suicide and she had given him a hug to say thanks. There was nothing more to it, but Lucas didn't believe her. Instead he put her in her place, pounding into her, day in and day out, hoping it would keep her in his grasp and make her stay. She always left and then always returned, so he viewed it as a success.

Eventually he grew bored with her as there was no hunt. She became too submissive and it lessened the excitement. Don't women know men like a chase?

5:10 p.m.

As Leona neared the door of the conference room on her way out for the day, she saw Garcia blocking her exit with her towering basketball frame. It seemed she wanted to talk to her, so Leona slowed. She didn't have the time or emotional space for her.

"In a rush?" Garcia said, looking down at Leona's contorted face. She'd never been good at hiding her thoughts.

"Um, no, I'm fine. I'm just on my way out and trying not to be late. I don't want to make the same mistake at my next job," she said with a laugh, trying to lighten the mood. "Got to be on time, you know?"

"You have another job?" Garcia asked.

Leona grimaced. McDonalds flashed before her eyes. *How could Garcia not remember she had another job?* The fact of the matter was that Leona had put this on her resume and spoken about it multiple times. It bothered her that her boss had so little understanding of what her workers' lives looked like.

"Yes, I work at McDonalds," she said finally, "...and I came from school before this. My life is quite a whirlwind actually, but I'm trying my best to make it all work out," she responded. In that moment she wanted to explain everything, as a well of fury rose up in her and danced for attention. She wanted to say that she had a thousand things to line up every morning before venturing out of her house, that very little of her life was in her control, that she had no idea how how to do anything she was doing, that her mom was depressed and her stepdad was missing, that men and the memory of her assault bothered her wherever she went, and that she was carrying her entire family and their financial well being on her shoulders. Instead, she remained quiet and looked up at Garcia.

"Yes, you do have quite an issue with time, don't you?" Garcia responded, ignoring her explanation.

It flustered Leona. "Did you need something?" she asked in a manner that was more direct than she had intended, clearing her throat and feeling the animal inside her dance in the mosh pit. She punched her elbows up and thrashed against the crowd. There had to be somewhere to get this angst out, somewhere safe. Her face reddened and her pulse began to quicken.

"No. I just wanted to say that besides the punctuality issue, you're doing a really good job," Garcia said.

Leona raised her eyebrows in surprise. "Oh" she responded in shock. She looked at her askance, assuming it was sarcasm or just the preface to something terrible, but her boss stared back at her as if it wasn't anything out of the ordinary.

"Yeah, I just want you to know that," Garcia continued as she pulled her dark straight hair in front of her shoulders, as if preparing to take a picture. "I know I'm hard on you, but it's because I see potential. You remind me of myself when I was your age.

"Ummm...thank you," Leona said, shocked by Garcia's sudden humanity and also surprised that she saw herself in her. *Hadn't she just thought that?* It made her shudder for a moment. "I appreciate the compliment."

"You'll get there, Leona," she continued. "Eventually you'll get where you want to be if you keep pushing. Don't let anything hold you down."

There was a tiny window opening and Leona saw a fraction of opportunity, so she pounced before it slammed shut. She knew bosses loved to be looked up to; egos enjoy being watered.

"Can I ask you something?" Leona prodded.

"Sure," Garcia answered with an openness that continued to throw her off as she talked. Leona noticed an intricate feather tattoo peeking out from the black silk of her boss's sleeve on her left arm. She'd never seen it before, and it piqued her curiosity.

She decided to go for it. "I've heard your story—how you made it from nothing, worked hard, and changed your family narrative—but I want to know how you actually did it. I mean in the day-to-day sense. How did you deal with the struggle?" she started. "The story sounds so simple—as if you didn't really waver much, but I'm sure that's not how it was."

"Yeah, it wasn't easy. It wasn't a direct line; it was twisted, and I failed multiple times which resulted in a lack of confidence but slowly it built its way back up. You have no idea how much harder I had to push because I was poor, and worse yet, a woman. No one took us seriously back then, so it was really tough to rise." She cleared her throat, reveling in the admiration. "But the important thing was that I didn't let anyone tell me who I was. I decided who I was and what I was going to be. Then I moved forward. Slowly but surely, I found myself with the life I wanted."

Leona thought about the irony in her statement, being that she had "made it" but was a generally horrible person to be around by all accounts.

"I relate with that," Leona responded. "I find myself doubting that I can do it every day, but I want success—freedom, really for myself and my family—more than anything else so I push myself as much as I can. It's painful though and sometimes I feel like it will never happen."

"It will, don't worry. And about freedom, it is what we all want," Garcia relayed.

"I guess that's true," Leona continued. "I want to get out of the mess I'm in and also I want to fight to make other peoples' lives better. My family is poor, and it doesn't seem like there's any way out. I'm in school but so far it hasn't changed anything. Every time something good happens, a new disaster seems to be right on its tail."

"Well, you have to push past that stuff, expect the worst, and put the doubt to bed. We all have this problem–negative self talk. You've got to put it in its place," she responded. "When I was younger, things kept going wrong all the time, believe me, and I just kept going. When I would get a 'no,' I had to learn to take it as a 'not yet.' There was no other option. It was either I kept at it or stayed stuck. What kind of choice is that?"

"Funny, my boyfriend and I always say that," Leona responded. "There's really no choice. It's either you get out or die trying."

"You've got a good head on your shoulders, Leona. You'll make it. I really think so," Garcia said, smiling. For a moment it almost felt like her boss was going to give her a hug, and she didn't know how she would respond if she did, but instead of leaning in, Garcia hardened herself again. "Now stop being late or I'm going to have to fire your ass!"

* * *

Leona stepped outside, feeling elated. She had just connected with Garcia for the first time and learned something that might help her. It felt good. Maybe Garcia wasn't that bad.

She seemed to think she was an asset—or at least she had said so. She wasn't the type to lie to make Leona feel good. That wasn't her style.

Leona felt around in her bag for her bus pass, rummaging through the mess of receipts and other junk. She'd been meaning to clean out her purse for a long time but had never gotten around to it, as it was just one more thing to do in a sea of things needing attention.

Where is my pass? she wondered, as her fingers did the work.

She felt a breeze and looked up for a moment, realizing that heat was beginning to recede slightly. It was nice. LA never seemed to cool down.

"You know what time it comes?" a middle aged woman asked, walking up to her as Leona continued to feel around in her bag.

"Uh, yeah, it should be here any minute...like in 5 minutes or so," she said. She moved things around some more, but it seemed her pass was nowhere to be found. Receipts and flyers, her wallet, trash and gum. No bus pass.

"Okay, thank you," the woman said, as she leaned against a pole, her heavy bags draped on her shoulders. "I couldn't find the schedule online. Everything is so complicated nowadays."

"Yeah, I know. It is, isn't it?" Leona answered in agreement, not looking up. Her fingers began to move more frantically, sensing impending doom. It wasn't there though, no denying it. She had to scramble. The evening stacked itself in front of her in a tall succession of flimsy mismatched cards. She opened her wallet to see if she could find enough change for the ride. Nothing much. There were a few quarters in her bag, but she needed $1.25 to board. She had already spent the money she had on cashews.

She *had* to get to McDonald's. A sense of urgency set in as she realized there was no way around begging. "Do you happen to have a quarter?" she asked the woman who had inquired earlier about the bus.

The woman opened her purse and looked in. "No, sorry. I haven't carried change in a long time, sweetie. Are you okay?"

"Yes, I think so. Thanks for checking," she said, furrowing her brow at the thought of having to ask someone else.

I can't be late. Not again, she thought. The anticipation of messing up when her day had already been so full of trouble sat in her mind. Anxiety began to pulse through her veins. Because there were so many unhoused people in the city, no one had much patience for panhandling and that's what she'd look like. She was afraid people would just think she was one of them and write her off. Self-pity washed over her, reaching every inch of her skin.

Her shoulders sank as she fell deeper. She had a habit of sitting and thinking instead of acting when she was in this situation, so that's what she did. One thing went wrong and everything fell back into chaos, scribbles all over the place like a child's art piece wanting to break free on a white wall.

Why does it still feel like this? She contemplated this idea for a moment and then shut her pity into a box as she pushed herself out. There was no time for it. *No more negative self talk*, she thought, thinking back to her talk with Garcia.

Maybe I can get out, she thought.

Her muscles felt tight as she lifted her arms to try to stretch. Would her wings work? It didn't seem like it, but she felt like she had to give it a try. Shrugging her shoulders, she opened up her chest, intent on lifting herself up and out of the mess, and began to flap. She would make it, no longer at the mercy of the transportation services or rapey men. She would be truly free. With this thought she rose off of the ground and made sure that her bag was fastened before she lifted off. As she ascended, the ground beneath her fell into a maze pattern and she could see everything for what it was: simple. A slow glitter formed under her and her entire life was covered in a golden haze.

But just as elation filled her body, her feet fell back to the ground. She looked around to see if anyone had noticed? A teenager with a skateboard leaned up against a wall and an elderly woman with a hunched back and a hair net holding a bag full of bananas stood nearby. Nothing had changed. Reality reentered her consciousness.

Who to ask? she thought. She decided to go with her instinct and straightened herself up in an attempt to look professional. Thanks to the blood stain on her elbow and the mark on her pants, it was harder than usual.

"Hi, I lost my bus pass, and I need some change to get onto the bus. Do you happen to have anything?" The elderly woman looked her up and down, and seeing her disheveled appearance, moved away, disturbed, without answering. Leona couldn't blame her.

She moved towards the teen. He made eye contact with her. "Yeah, I heard," he said, holding out money in his sweaty palm without making her ask. "How much do you need?"

"Seventy-five cents."

"No worries. I got you," he said as he handed her the change. "We all have those days."

"Thank you so much! You have no idea how much this saves me," she said, taking the money. "I hope this kindness finds its way back to you someday."

"It's all good. I'm happy to help."

She moved away and gave him some space, assuming that he probably didn't want to continue talking. Her heart felt warm. There was some good left in the world.

The big blue bus pulled to a stop next to her. She got on and found a seat, thankful for the humanity she had been shown. The teen sat across from her, intently listening to his music and tapping his skateboard to the beat with a carefree air about him. The bottom of his board was bright yellow with a drawing of a whiskey bottle on it. Two fish with mustaches danced around the alcohol. She wondered what his story was and wished she could do something nice for him.

A young man across from her wore a key on a gold chain around his neck, and it reminded her of Atzi's. Suddenly, she realized she hadn't seen it earlier.

Oh my god, she thought. *Not this...*

She frantically pulled her bag open and peered inside, frantically moving things around to get a better look of what was there. Atzi's key wasn't there. Her mind fell into panic. She quickly descended from her high in the sky, 'maybe everything will be okay' and 'wow my boss actually has a heart' to the thresholds of the underworld, River Styx and all. The dogs were hungry and waiting for her return, salivating as she got off the boat at the entrance of Hades. *I'm back again. Did you miss me?* She thought as she peered in the direction of the panting dogs.

In this moment, she called out to me:

Xochitl,

Just when it seemed like things were looking up, I lost the key: the one thing I have left of you and our family. You entrusted it to me. How could I be so stupid?

I wish you were here. What am I going to do? I'd do anything to have you back with me or at least help me find the key again. I know it's silly, but it made me feel like you were with me. It's been carrying your spirit the entire time. You'd probably laugh at that, but I believe it. Where are you?

This is too much. Help me please.

. . .

I wished nothing more than to give her a hug, or better yet the heirloom, at this moment. My love went out to her, and I moved closer. I don't think she saw me. I wanted to yell to her that she could do it–that it wasn't our key that gave her strength–it was her; she had the power.

All I could do was watch her fall apart.

5:21 p.m.

There were two rooms left to dismantle, and it was late. Usually 4p.m. was closing time, especially in the city when traffic would be an issue, but the accident and loss of their entire workforce was causing the day to drag.

"How long do you think we'll go?" Sergio asked. He knew his wife and kids were probably expecting him soon. He hadn't had the chance to stop again and communicate. "I need to get home."

"I don't know...until we're done, I guess," Lucas responded as he lifted some of the crown molding off of the walls and loaded it into a wheelbarrow. He smirked. "I'm sure they can live without you, Serg."

Suddenly, the worker who had passed out walked in. "Estamos trabajando?" He looked like a ghost but acted casual as if he hadn't just been incapacitated in the emergency room.

"Where did you come from?" Lucas asked as jumped to his feet and walked over to the man. "This is all your fault, you know. You forgot to turn the gas off, passed out, caused us to lose our guys. Now you walk back in here as if nothing happened?" he yelled as he moved in closer to the man's face. "You're responsible for all of this."

Sergio looked over at him in disbelief. "Don't be cruel. He came back. He must need the money. Just chill out." Lucas had been on edge all day and he'd had enough of it. "Plus, the guy could sue the company, you know. He got hurt on the job."

Lucas shot back at him. "No, he couldn't. This mother fucker is obviously clueless and illegal, so there's no threat here. He should own up for what he did and make up for it."

"So it was the gas, huh? When I asked you said you didn't know but it looks like you did."

Lucas cleared his throat, looked at the man in desperation, and then turned back to Sergio. "I mean, I don't know... maybe. Probably. Either way, it was his fault for being an idiot and not double checking. He was standing right by the valve," he yelled. "And look at him," he said as he pivoted, "he's still standing there dumb after I told him to get back to work."

"He doesn't understand you," Sergio shot back.

"Well then translate already," Lucas said with a gruff voice. "We need to get out of here at some point tonight and we're never going to if we don't get moving."

"You're a dick," Sergio said as he looked Lucas straight in the eyes, "and I wouldn't work with you if I didn't have two little girls to support."

"Well, lucky for me you need the money."

6:05 p.m.

Leona walked quickly to the break room to see if she could clock in before Marcus noticed that she was late. She placed her bag into the locker and tried to slam it shut, but it swung back at her face, just as the day had. She caught it just before it hit.

Trash was everywhere, but she pushed it aside to sit down for a moment and breathe. It looked like Marcus was on break and had stepped out, so she quickly called Carlos. She had to tell him about Atzi's key. He was the only one who would make her feel better.

"Hey babe," he answered in haste. "What's up? I'm on break right now, so I only have a second."

"Oh okay, I've had an insane day," she said as she let out a long exhale.

"What happened?" he asked. She could picture his caring face and it brought a momentary sense of peace.

"A better question is what didn't happen."

"It can't be that bad."

"Yes, it can. It is. I didn't tell you a lot of what had happened earlier because I was so sad about you not getting into UCLA, but it's been a freakishly crazy day. Some idiot tried to grab me at the bus stop, so I ran to Hope Street to try to catch the other one, but the bus had already left, of course. Then I hustled to the metro in a last-ditch effort to get to class on time, but I was late regardless. So annoying. And I was starving all morning because I forgot to eat breakfast..."

"Leona, I told you to grab something. I knew you'd be rushed," he interrupted.

"Yeah, well...you were right. So anyways, class sucked. This girl was trying to argue that we didn't really need to talk about rape because it wasn't a problem and everyone was just sitting there..."

"Seriously? Some people are so stupid."

"I know. She was relentlessly ignorant."

"Did you set her straight?" He asked, already knowing the answer. She knew he loved her fire.

"Yes, I did. Something shifted in me today. I just can't handle sitting still. It's like a cave inside of me opened up and let all of the dragons rush out," she said as she laughed into the phone. "And you should have seen the woman's boyfriend. Such a jerk. He was rubbing her neck the whole time as if he controlled her mouth. He even called me a stupid feminist as he walked out. His girlfriend just giggled. It was disgusting"

"I know the type," he said.

"But that's not the worst part. There's more. The bus to Garcia's was horrible. It stopped abruptly for some reason, and I flew forward and dropped all of my shit on the floor. I scratched my elbow, got a huge stain on my pants, but most importantly, I lost my key."

"That's okay, I'll just let you in later," he said, surprised that she was so upset about that.

"No, Los...Atzi's..." she said with fervor. "I lost our heirloom."

He listened, knowing how much it meant to her. Once she was done, he asked. "Are you okay?"

"Not really," she sighed, finally letting herself feel. Her eyes welled up. Carlos calmed her like an escape from sweltering heat but he also made her drop her guard which meant had a hard time holding back from her tears. "I'm such an idiot," she paused as she let herself cry. "I didn't notice it was gone until I was looking for my bus pass, which is also gone, of course. So much for efficiency. You know I put everything together so I won't lose it," she said, laughing lightly about the irony and trying to lift her mood.

"Sorry, baby. I got you. I'll be home tonight when you get off, and I'll make you feel better," he said in a comforting manner. "I'm sorry you lost the key. I know how much it means to you."

"Thanks sweetie," she said slowly and then realized the time. "I've gotta go. My shift has already started. I don't want Marcus to see me slacking. Hopefully everything will be okay."

He cleared his throat and then paused, saying "Wait, did you hear from UCLA?"

"Oh, I don't know," she said as she checked her email. "I've been so busy. I haven't checked again."

"Okay, well make sure you let me know as soon as you see something. I want to celebrate with you."

"Yeah, whatever," she said. "I'm not sure I still want to go."

"Shut up please. No more of that."

"Okay, fine. Talk to you later," she said.

Leona changed into her black polo shirt quickly and walked to the front to start her shift. She still had the dark stain on her pant leg, but overall, she was feeling a bit better after telling Carlos everything. Although it was mostly bad news, she realized that she was still standing and because of this fact she felt a little bit stronger, braver even.

I liked seeing Leona smile and recognize her own strength. It was empowering. Her comments about not going to UCLA were a bit concerning, but we can't blame her. It's not great that she's holding so close to Carlos, but I can't blame her. It's difficult to do it alone. We shouldn't judge each other for leaning on others here and there. After all, humans are not islands. Nor should we be. That's one of the greatest flaws American culture has forced upon us, the idea that we need to do everything on our own. We are social animals.

"What's up?" her friend, Esmeralda, yelled as she saw her and gave her a hug. "I didn't see you come in."

"Yeah, I was hiding because I am late," she said.

Esmeralda was five years younger than Leona, but she was an old soul. She reminded Leona of her aunt Cecilia. They had the same energy: lively and sarcastic, fight not flight. It was obvious that Esmeralda looked to Leona for direction and inspiration, and she emanated the energy of growth. Leona looked to her for a different kind of strength—a raw one that Esmeralda seemed to carry naturally. Reciprocity bloomed between the two.

"Bad day," Leona said with a sideways glance. "Everything that could go wrong did. ...well, not everything, but you catch my drift. It's been a wicked crazy day, and it all started with a horrible nightmare. The day was shot from the moment I opened my eyes."

"La vida loca," Esmeralda said jokingly. "Don't I know it."

"Isn't that a gang thing?" Leona questioned, with a side

glance. She felt like messing around, hoping it would change the energy around her.

"Well, yeah silly, but I didn't mean it that way," Esmeralda answered.

"I know, I know," Leona asserted. "Where's Marcus?"

"He had a meeting about punctuality with Corporate. I'm sure he'll come back and be all strict like he usually is after they drill him about something."

They laughed for a minute about the attention their boss paid to arbitrary details. Overall, he was a considerate and supportive manager, but much like other people who held high—yet not really important—positions, he liked to exert his dominance over his subordinates to make himself feel better. They still liked him, but they also enjoyed teasing him.

"Yeah, being on time is *so* important." Leona laughed. "Doesn't matter how you serve the customers, but make sure you're not even a moment late."

"You know it," Esmeralda said, her round face scrunched into a grin. She was one of the happiest people Leona knew, and she admired her for it. It's not that her life was simple—in fact, it was as complicated as anyone's—but it was the way she decided to deal with the rotten eggs she was served that was admirable. Esmeralda laughed at the chaos and just moved forward. Leona didn't know how to do that.

She gave her a quick side hug and said, "You always make my day better."

"Of course I do." responded Esmeralda. "Now let's get out there. It's going to be a good night."

"Is it, though?" Leona questioned.

"Shut up with that pessimism," she said.

The night was busier than usual. There was a smattering of families huddled for a quick cheap meal, a teen couple interlocked in the escape of embrace, and some singletons keeping themselves busy on their phone: all of them mixed up in a long line together. Most of the crowd looked tired to one degree or another. Leona sighed as she thought of the long night ahead. Her exhaustion was sitting heavily on her now and it felt like she had been doing all of this for years. She had, actually. Initially she'd planned to only work at McDonalds for a year or two while she finished up community college, but when that got dragged out, so did her time making burgers.

We all take more time than originally planned. Life is unreliable–it's only our ego that allows us to have the misconception that we're the deciders of our fate. And sometimes these long-drawn out sections of our lives turn out to be something we needed all along.

When I was Leona's age I was just learning how to be a human. I remember falling over and over again, and then getting up to lick my wounds. Hell, I got married early and then got pregnant shortly afterward. Luckily I had someone to help me get to know myself. My mom was a sweet-tempered pixie of a woman. She would watch me do my own thing, and only offer advice when I asked. It was the best type of parenting for a person like me–I've always been quite an independent soul. When needed, she would come in with a loving hand and questions. 'Do you think that worked out?' 'How do you think you might change things next time?' That sort of thing. It was perfect. I could lean on her if needed, but she wasn't pulling or pushing, trying to get my attention. So many parents keep their kids dependent, but it teaches them nothing.

All of the self inflicted and external turmoil actually got me where I wanted. After learning to pursue through the weeds, I was able to get into music and make something of myself. I didn't see it then. At that time it just looked like brambles, but I was actually getting somewhere. Hopefully Leona sees that she is getting somewhere–there is an end to the madness.

Leona leaned on me a bit here and there before I passed, but I tried to stay back unless she needed something, hoping my technique helped her to see how strong she was. I guess the real test is to see how you do when you don't have many people to rely on. Now she's in that position. I mean she has Carlos, but he's still young. Seems like she's doing okay, maybe even great, despite the circumstances. All I can do is watch and try to send her some hints of goodness, maybe place something magical in her path. I don't have the same effect as I did before, but I do have something.

6:14 p.m.

Monsters don't grow strong until something provokes them into full form. Until this happens they are shadow creatures, just trying on different costumes to see which fits best. They cause violence along the way, but it's nothing like the chaos they'll unfold once they find themselves.

Lucas turned sour well before Cynthia left but it was his mother's sudden exodus that cemented it. Before she disappeared she told him of the pain that ached inside of her, that it was partially his to carry. Not only had she been beaten by The General, but she knew her son, the one she'd tried to protect when he was young, had watched her in pain, almost ghost-like, without stepping in. Lucas thought she hadn't known he was there, but she knew very well what was brewing underneath his skin.

Why didn't you ever step in?

What do you mean?

I know you knew.

Knew what?

Knew I was crumbling. Knew I needed help. Your father is twice as strong and angry as I am.

When his mother confronted him on this he stood silent. She could see that her son was hollow, empty in every capacity, and even more, she knew there was nothing left to figure out. A mother sees her son, whether he wants to be seen or not. There's something about that bond that doesn't shade easily. It's thicker than bones but equally transparent.

Her conversation with Lucas died there on the tracks that day, before even taking off. There was nothing to be said as no answer would ever explain his apathy, his cowardice. He wasn't even sure it was cowardice as very little in him wanted to act. Why didn't he want to save her? Why didn't he care more? She had been a good mom, the best she could be under the circumstances. Her main focus had been ducking The General's punches but when she wasn't in the line of fire, she had taken care of the boys. Somehow though, Lucas' heart didn't warm much in her presence. Instead, he found himself to resemble a statue.

Lucas thought about his inaction often and the guilt ate at him. It wasn't true guilt, but rather the guilt of not feeling much.

His younger brother had been the only one who ever stopped The General.

Tyler was always better than his brothers.

Tyler was his mom's favorite and who could blame her?

Everyone knew this to be true, and that's why when he left, she had to as well. She couldn't live in a house full of animals, even if they were her own.

Lucas didn't know where she was now, but he did know something: he knew there was no longer anything meaningful in that house. Joseph and The General replaced all that was good with darkness soon after she left and it was almost as if she'd never been there. He told himself it was better that way. They were all more themselves. Real men.

That was until Joseph's girlfriend moved in. Lately, his brother had been getting soft. Lucas noticed the girl getting a lot of what she wanted. *Will you stop by and grab me a coffee on your way home from the golf range? When are you coming home?* That sort of stuff, and Joseph seemed to be folding like a beach chair. He said he never would, and it shocked Lucas to see him cower. He thought his brother would never change, but somehow it was happening. Maybe everyone got limp as they grew older. He hoped to never turn into mush like them, being blown into smithereens by the whisper of a lover. Last week, Joseph, the top dog under The General, actually said, 'Well, my girlfriend wants to' or something like that which was so surprising coming from him. Inside, Lucas feared that he himself might one day crumble.

"Who gives a fuck? What happened to the guy who does what he wants and doesn't let anyone stop him? What happened to that guy" Lucas said.

"You've always been an idiot," his brother responded. "Haven't you noticed that our lives suck? Think about it, mom's gone, Tyler's gone, and it's just us three living in the shitty house in Riverside, and even worse, with our dad. We're grown ass men. I think I finally understand why we've been stuck here for so long–we're the dumb ones. It's not them, it's us!" Joseph shot back. "I don't know about you, but I'm not going to live that way. I want to make something of my life, have a wife, a family...love."

At this, Lucas was overwhelmed with guilt and disgusted. He punched his brother in the face as hard as he could and memories of his violence with Tyler resurface. Joseph fell back onto the couch and then got up and pushed him with all of his might. He held him up against the wall, with his hand on Lucas' neck, keeping him steady.

"What the fuck is wrong with you?" Joseph yelled as he bled from his nose and tried to keep Lucas from getting to him. "This is exactly what I'm talking about. Grow the fuck up."

Joseph was evaporating. He would be the one, he decided. He would be the only soldier standing and his father would notice that the other two were weak. He laughed to himself and felt full as he looked his brother in the face. He had won; he was the only man left. Joseph let go of him as he felt the anger flow out of his body.

"You're an idiot, you know. It's time to get a life and stop pushing your way around everywhere. It's time to become a real man," Joseph spat as he backed away.

At this, Lucas lunged at him again. "I am. You wouldn't know the first thing about it."

"Okay, loser. You're right. You're the man," Joseph said as he disappeared into the hall. "You're the big guy." Joseph said, as he walked away from his little brother.

"You fucking know it," Lucas said, rubbing his neck.

After that night, Lucas saw more and more signs of Joseph wavering and evaporating into the kind of man he saw everywhere now. Weak. accommodating. When his girlfriend came home late, he met her with a hug and smile instead of anger. He never saw him lay a hand on her, and she was quite out of control from Lucas' perspective. She needed to be put in her spot. *Didn't he see that?* They always say if you don't control your women, they will control you.

7:15 p.m.

The dining room had thinned out, and Leona finally had time to chat with Esmeralda. They had been slammed since she walked in.

"I don't feel good," Leona said. "It's like I'm hollow. I can't get myself into a better headspace. Maybe it's because I lost my swallow key."

"Wait, you did? " Esmeralda asked. "Oh no, I know how much you love that thing. You're never without it. What happened?"

"On the bus, I guess... when I fell," Leona explained. "It must have fallen out with the other stuff. I can't believe I was such a fool to not check my bag better. I was honestly just so tired and pissed off that I didn't want to do anything."

"I'm so sorry."

"It's fine," she said, not believing it herself. "It's all good. Can't do anything about it now, I guess."

"Maybe you can go back and check the bus," Esmeralda offered. "You never know..."

"Yeah, maybe," Leona answered. She suddenly wanted nothing more than to change the subject. The thought of the lost key sitting somewhere on the bus floor, probably being trampled on, was too much for her to begin to consider. "So how was it before I got in today? Anything happen?"

"Mostly good," Esmeralda answered. She seemed to have picked up on Leona's desire to move on. "...the only thing was some mean guy was pissed off that his fries were wet," she answered, laughing. "He was such a jerk about it, but they probably were. Johnny is on fries, so..."

Leona rolled her eyes. Johnny was always high, but somehow he flew under the radar. "Yeah, who knows what he's doing over there."

At this, they both glanced back at Johnny, who was happily, albeit slowly, working on fries, batch after batch. He didn't seem to have a care in the world. Sometimes Leona thought he was the smart one. He didn't go for much and seemed happy with his life. She wished she could be that way, content, but then again she didn't.

"Did you see him on Saturday? I think he had more weed in him than food." Esmeralda said. "I'm surprised the customers never say anything. It's like he's invisible. Bloodshot eyes, slurred speech, but somehow never gets in trouble."

"I think everyone just feels bad for him. He's sweet... stupid, but sweet."

"Leo!" Esmeralda hit her arm and laughed. They were like middle schoolers again.

"Sorry, sorry," she conceded. "I like Johnny," Leona said, trying to save face.

"It's too late. You already showed your true colors," Esmeralda said, laughing. "You can't just say 'I like Johnny' after throwing him to the dogs."

A young girl with a Hannah Montana shirt walked up to the

counter and looked straight at Leona. She had an "I'm trying to be brave" look on her face.

"Need help?" Leona asked, as she leaned on the sticky counter in order to get down on the girl's level. She looked to be around five or six years old and had one long thick braid that reached down to her waist. She was very out of place in the middle of the city—almost like she was part of a cult and had wandered into the outside world for the first time.

"I don't know where my mommy is," she said with a slight tremor in her voice and a ting of a southern accent. "She was here, but now she's gone, and..." Tears began to well up in the girl's eyes.

"Okay, okay...no worries." Leona could tell she was on the verge of breaking down, so she leapt into action, recognizing the neglect.

Moving around the counter, Leona grabbed the little girl's hand and took charge of the situation. She wanted to make her feel like everything was going to be okay. "We will find your mom," she said. "Be brave...that's what we girls do. We bravely face problems."

Despite the bravery spiel, Leona feared the worst. She had heard about this kind of thing happening, especially recently. There had been a string of people dropping their kids off at restaurants and walking away. That any parent could abandon his or her child was beyond her understanding, but it was a fact nevertheless. Some people just didn't care.

"What's your favorite song?" Leona asked the little girl, trying to distract her from her worry and pull out the happy child that she assumed existed inside.

"Um, I don't know." She looked up nervously. The tactic wasn't working, but Leona knew she had to keep trying.

"C'mon, you have to have a favorite song. Everyone has one," she prodded.

"I guess 'Party in the USA...'" she said and then began to

hum the tune. It seemed to lighten her mood a bit. There was a small ounce of hope in her dark eyes as she allowed the song to trickle out of her mouth. For a moment, she became the child she should have been able to be, free and innocent, again.

"I know that one! Let's sing it together as we check everything out," Leona offered as she walked the girl around the dining room.

"Okay," she said, seeming to let her anxiety lift a bit.

They sang quietly as they circled the restaurant, walking around so that the girl could see if she recognized anyone. They probably looked strange together, Leona thought.

The girl's mother was nowhere to be found.

Suddenly, Leona had a hunch to check the restroom. She couldn't imagine a person would go to the bathroom and leave their young child in McDonald's at night—or at any time, for that matter—but perhaps they didn't have a choice. Maybe it was a grandparent or something like that and the whole thing was an accident.

"Did your mom go to the bathroom?" she asked. She could see her younger self in the little girl's eyes, and she immediately remembered how she felt when her mom fell to pieces after her dad left. It was frightening. Leona had been much older than this girl, but most of the time, she felt like a dead fish hanging on the line, wiggling slightly as life drained out of her, hoping for salvation.

The young girl held Leona's hand anxiously and responded," I don't think so."

"Well, let's just check. Maybe she's in there."

Leona grasped the metal handle of the door and pulled while maintaining a hold on the girl's hand. Leona saw some feet under one of the stalls.

"Did you happen to lose someone?" she said loudly. "I have a little girl here who is looking for her mom."

The woman shuffled her worn tennis shoes for a moment and then Leona heard a sigh.

"Yeah?" Her raspy voice echoed in the stall. "Charlotte?," she said.

At the sound of her mother's voice the girl began to cry and yelp. "Mama! Where were you? I was so scared," she said as she shook.

"Damn it, Charlotte!" the mother yelled with a snarl, ignoring the question. "I told you to stay put." Her anger was palpable.

The woman flushed the toilet abruptly and moved towards the door. When she saw her mom, the flood gates opened. She seemed to know what was coming.

Leona continued to hold the girl's hand, reluctant to let her go to her mother. She didn't know what to do—didn't know what to expect from this woman who was yelling at her scared little girl. *Should someone like that be raising a child?* she thought. Her gut told her to call the police, but she was afraid it might do more harm as she could be sent to somewhere even more unsafe. There were so many stories about kids being abused or neglected after someone called CPS; she wasn't sure it was the way to go.

A wiry woman walked out. Her hair was dark with bleached blonde tips, and her shirt was baggy and worn. Leona noticed a smudge of what looked like powder on the woman's neck, which made her wonder.

"Come here!" she yelled as Charlotte ran over to her and hugged her belly, shaking. "You're fine. Stop crying. I told you I was going to go to the bathroom," she said as she held her daughter's face to her abdomen. "Don't be a baby."

"You didn't say..." Charlotte said as tears ran down her face. "I looked up and you were gone..." She was unsuccessfully trying to control herself. "I thought you left again."

The word "again" hung like a noose.

"You're okay. You ARE okay," the mother commanded before taking Charlotte by the hand. "Now thank this nice lady and let's go." The woman looked up at Leona with a strained smile.

Leona met her gaze with anger. *How could she do this? Will Charlotte be okay? Should I do something?* There were no answers for these questions. The woman seemed to be agitated. *At what point should a person step in?* she thought, trying to ascertain what she should do.

"Thanks" Charlotte said, as she looked at Leona.

Leona decided to push back against the mother. It didn't feel right just moving on and pretending nothing happened. Something had to be done. She wanted to make sure Charlotte would be safe. "Is everything okay with you?" she asked the mother. "She could have been kidnapped, you know? It's not safe to leave kids alone around here—or anywhere, for that matter. Your daughter was super brave, but also so scared. Anyone could have taken her. Do you understand this?"

Tarana Burke

I don't want to be brave; I want to be free.

* * *

Tarana Burke, founder of the Me Too Movement, was raped at the age of seven and then again at nine. In both of these instances she blamed herself for the assault; she had been told that good girls didn't let boys touch them in their private places. Therefore, because it happened to her, she assumed it was her fault. It took her years to realize that she had been the victim.

When she read *I Know Why the Caged Bird Sings* by Maya Angelou, and learned about the rape that Angelou had endured at the hands of her step-father, she came to the understanding that what had happened to her was not an isolated incident, and additionally, that it wasn't her fault. Burke saw herself in Angelou, being that she was a strong black woman and had continued to do well despite her assault.

In 2006, Burke coined the phrase Me Too as a way for victims (mostly women and girls of color) to share their stories about sexual violence and get support from their community. She had spent decades listening to peoples' stories about being sexually assaulted and the difficulty they had in getting justice and finding a way out of the despair that accompanies rape.

Following the movie producer, Harvey Weinstein's, rape and harassment charges, the actress Alyssa Milano tweeted the hashtag #MeToo to try to grow the conversation about the topic and give victims a voice. As a response, users filled the Internet with personal stories of rape. When Burke saw this she was concerned that all of her hard work would be ignored and that women of color would be brushed aside as they had been previously. She was also concerned that the Internet was a dangerous place for women to tell their stories, being that there is so much harassment online.

After careful consideration, she realized that something positive was forming out of the hashtag movement, being that it gave people a voice, and a sense of community, when they had previously felt alone in their horror . She decided to tell her own story, in a memoir called *Unbound*, to make sure the stories of black and brown women were heard, and steer the conversation towards healing and accountability. As of 2018, the hashtag #MeToo had been used over 19 million times showing that sexual assault is a pervasive problem in America.

7:24 p.m.

The mother stared at Leona, unfazed, and then tried to move past her.

"It's none of your business," she said.

This response infuriated Leona. *How can a parent be so neglectful?*

"What's wrong with you?" Leona continued. She couldn't believe what was coming out of her mouth, but she said it before she could think. Instead of holding back, she found herself in the middle of a confrontation. She hadn't had the intention of sticking her head out; it just happened.

The woman stared at her aghast as if no one had ever questioned her before and took a step towards Leona, who braced herself for whatever was about to come her way.

She could take it. She would fight for this girl. I felt my own chest inflating as I wished I could move down there and help her. She didn't need me, but I wanted to just the same. It seemed she had taken on a strength of her own. I thought about all of the women I've known who have fought to defend others. The first person who came to mind was Dolores Huerta, the leader of the farm workers association, who along with Caesar Chavez, stood up for the underdogs. Leona looked like Huerta at that moment.

"Stay out of it, young lady" the woman said as she towered over Leona. "My daughter is fine. Thank you for helping her, but please don't think you have the right to tell me how to parent. Do you have a child?"

"No, but..."

"But nothing," she continued. "You have no idea how to do this."

"Okay, but leaving a young girl alone in a restaurant at night, especially in this part of town, isn't safe. She was really scared." She paused to breathe. "It's super irresponsible. Someone could have assaulted or taken her, and it's your job to protect her." She looked down at Charlotte, who looked back at her. A slight smile began to form on the girl's lips despite the tears. Their confidence was growing in unison.

"This is ridiculous!" the woman said as she leaned in towards Leona and gripped her daughter's hand, making her squirm in discomfort. "I don't need to hear this from you. Where is your manager?"

Leona realized that she had opened a window that she wouldn't be able to shut, but she was proud to have done it. Someone needed to stand up for the girl and make her mother act better. She was so tired of people being overlooked. Kids shouldn't have to fight alone; no one should. Hopefully this would be the last of her mother's "accidents."

Charlotte smiled at Leona with a red face and soft tears that were still seeping out of her eyes slowly. It seemed the two of them had a secret understanding, and with this, Leona felt a sense of hope for her. And then, right on cue, she and Charlotte skipped out of the restaurant and ran into the beautifully flowering woods as swallows danced around their heads and deer came up to join the happy pair. Music played from a far away band and their hearts were full. No more sadness would come to them. All would be well. All women, mothers, sisters, daughters, and friends would live a lovely life without hardship or pain. No woman would ever hurt again. And the men wouldn't have a chance, because all women would protect each other. Especially the mothers: they would be the most respected of all.

Instead, Leona stared the woman down and then shifted to look at Charlotte with love. She said, "You were really brave. I'm proud of you. I told you everything would be alright. You deserve to be safe. If you ever need anything, I am here. Remember that. You're not alone in this world."

"Manager, now!" the woman howled, shaking her head back and forth and stomping her feet as if she might lunge at Leona. At this point, a few customers were staring at them, but Leona didn't care. She ached for justice, and she realized she had the strength to stick her neck out. In fact, she liked how it felt.

"I'll get him," Leona answered calmly. "Please take care of this sweet child. You're all that she has," she said as she walked over to get Marcus, who was sitting in the break room playing pool on his phone. She gave him a quick rundown of what had happened.

"Shit, Leona. Should we call the cops?" he asked.

"Maybe, but tell them what? That a mother left her child at the table while she went to the restroom?"

"Yeah, good point. They'll laugh."

"That's what I was thinking. They won't know that the girl was frantic and alone for what seemed like forever. I think the mom might be on drugs too."

"Great, but you know we don't know that."

"True," she agreed. There was no way to prove it. "But she had white powder on her neck, and she didn't open up the bathroom door for an absurd amount of time."

"It could have been sugar or powder or something."

"Yeah, I'm sure it was sugar," Leona said.

7:38 p.m.

"Do you think he'll stay quiet about this?" Scotty asked. "I mean we can't have him shooting his mouth off and ruining things."

"I know," Lucas replied. "Honestly, Serg is a pain in the neck, a rule follower. It's like he's got his wife on his shoulder or something. He's a great worker but I'm not sure if he'll lie for the job."

"Well, figure it out," Scotty continued. "We've got to do something in case it comes out. You know Sergio's cousin works for the company too, right?"

"Yeah," Lucas said, clearing his throat. "I wonder if he already suspects something? He was acting strange earlier.""

"Nah, I don't think so," Scotty said. "His cousin has been busy on 2nd all day working under Carlos."

Lucas paused, looking through the doorway at Sergio as he stood there talking to the worker. Surprisingly, the man seemed to be in good enough spirits, despite his trip to the emergency room. This made Lucas feel better. Maybe everything would be okay.

"I think we're good. We'll finish up here–it shouldn't take too long–and then I'll let you know," Lucas replied.

"Cool, text me before you leave. I want to make sure we're ready for tomorrow. We have to get an early start. It's gonna be a long day. The guys should be there to demo at like 8 a.m., as early as the city will let us begin."

Lucas walked off the job site and out of ear shot.

"One more thing," he said. "I think we can guarantee Sergio's silence," he paused, choosing his words carefully. He didn't know how far Scotty would be willing to go and didn't want to come off as manipulative. That was the last thing he needed.

"I'm listening..." Scotty replied.

"How about offering him a promotion, like a chance to move into some type of supervisor position for a future job? That would probably keep him in our good graces. Just the thought of making more money usually shuts people up when they are considering being a whistleblower. It's a lot to risk."

"True. You're smart. That's why I like having you. You think on your feet, Luke," Scotty said in haste. "I think that's a great idea. I'll meet you guys tonight after work and make sure things are clear."

Lucas sighed, thankful that he hadn't stuck his neck out only to find there was a guillotine awaiting him.

"Okay, I'll be in touch," he said and hung up with Scotty. He felt tall and strong, even competent for once.

When Lucas walked back into the warehouse Sergio was pulling an ornate fountain off the wall. It looked as if it was made in the 1920s during the art deco era. Some musty water splashed out of the basin but he ignored it. He seemed intent on moving it. The rich blue tile of the fountain fell away as the golden bosom of the woman in the fountain glistened.

"Need some help?" Lucas asked. "Where's the cholo?"

Sergio glared at him. *Who does this fucker think he is?* He thought. At that moment he wanted to shove Lucas' face into the fountain, but instead he settled himself, reminding himself it wasn't worth it.

"Not sure," he replied. "He was in the back room, but I haven't seen him for a few minutes. Are you going to help me with this or what? This would look nice in my backyard if you don't think the company would want it. My wife loves this kind of stuff."

"Your wife? Like I said, you're a slave to that woman," Lucas joked, as he helped him dislodge it. "But sure, we don't have to ask anyone. Just take it," he said, wanting to give him everything he desired as it might help him to stay quiet.

Sergio lifted it up and walked it out the door, leaving a trail of water behind him.

"Hey," Lucas called out as he walked to the back of the room and looked into the settling darkness. "Where is that guy? We've had enough of his mistakes today. It's time to finish up and get out of here."

"Not sure," Sergio responded. "Let's get out of here."

"Okay, good. I'll let Scotty know to meet us for a bite. We need to talk about tomorrow, and I owe you some grub. It's been a long and stressful day."

8:02 p.m.

Leona shut the door in the freezer and stood in awe of her own strength. Before today, it was so unusual for her to stand up and speak. She'd often felt like a brittle branch, so ready to snap, but now it seemed she was thickening and healthy. It seemed the desire to become an advocate was flowing into her. Although what she had done was uncomfortable, it was right. It fit well, felt good, and looked sharp on her.

Even if the mother was upset—and even if the woman didn't have any intention of harming her daughter—she still shouldn't have left her alone. Who will protect the children if not their own parents? Now, at least, Charlotte knew there were people in the world who would stand up for her, she thought.

As she worked with icy cold fingertips, she heard a bit of yelling, so she propped open the door to listen.

"I understand. I understand. Well, she had the best of intentions, but I hear your complaint," Marcus said.

As she listened to the conversation, she smiled to herself.

. . .

The freezer felt refreshing after her fiery rebuke and she thought about her own mother. There was so much to be desired in their relationship. She hadn't been there for Leona when she needed her the most and it made everything so much harder. But then again, her grandmother hadn't been there for Miranda when *she* had needed her either. It was a never ending cycle of neglect.

One of the cooks walked into the fridge, looking for a bin of lettuce, and nodded in her direction. "Some lady is screaming out there," he said. "You're safer here."

Leona laughed and responded, "Yeah, it's my fault too. She was yelling at me first and then wanted to talk to Marcus. Poor guy."

"What happened?" Joseph asked.

"She left her little girl in the dining room without supervision, and I thought she'd been abandoned, so I helped her find her mom."

"So, why is she yelling?" he asked while standing in front of her and holding the freezer door open.

"Maybe because I told her she was irresponsible," Leona answered as she raised her eyebrows. She knew this sounded bad. "And I made sure the little girl, Charlotte is her name, felt like someone cared about her. I guess the mom didn't like that.

"Damn Girl, that's a lot," he said as he propped the door open. "It's always good to stand up for the kids though. They can't do it themselves."

"Yeah, that's what I was thinking. I feel bad for Marcus but."

"Don't feel too bad. This is why he gets paid the big bucks," the friend responded.

"You know he makes next to nothing, right?" Leona prodded.

Joseph seemed unaware. "Well, he makes more than me," he said. "So much more so I don't feel bad.

Leona thought about everything and in this moment she decided she could never go back to being on the sidelines. No more taking it. No more sitting back. She would fight for herself and others.

Maybe this is the type of law I should practice, she thought. *Maybe I should fight for people who can't do so themselves. Yeah, that feels right.*

Rebellion began to form on her tongue, and she whispered her favorite word under her breath: *Basta.*

No one could hear her, but it didn't matter.

I'd like to take some credit for this. Leona can't have all of it–okay, well maybe she deserves most of it, but still it must be known that I'd been pouring all of my knowledge, and what I could muster of my strength, into her since she was a little twig. I knew, or at least I hoped, that at some point she'd find herself in a spot where she'd be stronger and able to stand up for herself. It was so great to see her taking a risk for Charlotte. It was as if she was standing up for herself, but decades later. That little girl had such a resemblance to her. It was striking.

Of course she couldn't see it because people don't see themselves clearly, but I definitely recognized it. Things are always clearer from a distance. *Isn't that what they say?*

I first saw this type of growth in my sweet Cecilia before her death. She was weak as a child and didn't know how to fight for herself but then everything turned. It happened in the same sort of way too, like the unfolding of pages in a book. The more you turn, the harder it is to keep the book open to the front; at some point, at a critical mass, the book falls over to the back cover and slams shut. This is how my girls are. They struggle until they don't. And then, in that bright light, they begin to shine so brightly that no one can ignore it.

I think we can all do this if prompted. If each woman took on the effort of encouraging another, the world would be full of stronger, more confident, kind and intelligent people. We could end this imbalance and really change things. We could take the book from the hands of the patriarchy and turn it to the page we like instead of having it shoved into our faces mid chapter.

Knowing Leona, this transformation would not end soon–once she gets going, she's like a fire. Suddenly, I thought of RBG and what I had written about her to Leona years before in one of my letters. Maybe that was what prompted Leona into law? I wasn't sure, but either way I was glad I had told her about the feminist icon. I remembered how the judge pushed back against every sexist, demeaning case that came before her. When she first came to the bench she was up against all kinds of gender discrimination and had to prove herself. I always loved her because of her fight for all of the women in this country. I saw that she believed in herself and didn't let anyone overlook her. She was competent and proud. I had written about all of this and sent it to Leona years ago. I hoped she saw the parallels in her own life. Although her triumphs were smaller in scale she was demonstrating similar strength in her ability to stand up against injustice even if it wasn't expected of her.

With newfound confidence, Leona put gloves on and got back into her work. She needed to get more hash browns to help the staff prepare for the morning shift, but they were stacked in boxes all the way up to the ceiling like the Tower of Babel.

This would normally throw her into a cynical mood, but for the first time in ages, she felt like she could conquer anything.

"She's gone," Marcus said as he peeked his head into the freezer.

"So how did it go?" she asked.

"I don't know. How do these things ever go?" Marcus responded. "I hope the little girl will be okay."

"I feel like we should have done more," Leona said.

"What more could we have done?" he inquired, to which Leona shrugged.

When Leona got back up to the front, Esmeralda was helping an elderly man in a cowboy hat with his order. He was complaining about how he remembered the menu differently, insisting that it must have changed. She glanced sideways and let out a sigh of relief to see Leona.

"Where did you go?" Esmeralda asked. "I saw you talking to that dumbass, then Marcus appeared, and you were gone."

"He put me in the freezer while he dealt with her," she answered. "I can't believe she left her kid out here all alone."

"Yeah, so stupid," responded Esmeralda. "They really should make you take a test to have a child."

"Or better yet, make birth control free," Leona said. "You shouldn't need to be wealthy to prevent pregnancy. I doubt that lady wanted a little one anyway."

"That's why they need to make people take a test. *Can you feed your child? Is it wrong to leave your child unattended?* Things like that—just the basics. We've got to do better."

"True, but think about it—wouldn't that be one more way they would control us? You know how those fascists are—they're already trying to make choices for us. Look what they're trying to do with Roe v. Wade."

"God, that's true," Esmeralda responded, letting go of a

huge exhale. "Maybe a test is a bad idea. We can't give them any more power."

With this thought, a million men marched in a line holding a lone woman in shackles–'we will decide what you do with your body.' Their boots stomped the ground like drums and their somber faces took on that of cockroaches. Darkness fell as the autocratic leader spoke from a podium about keeping the order and the purity of traditional norms, and all of that nonsense. Leona shook herself back into reality.

"You alright?" Esmeralda asked, peering into her empty face.

"Yeah, we definitely can't give them any more power," she responded.

8:12 p.m.

"Where did the guy go?" Scotty asked as he exited his truck and walked over to Lucas's window. He leaned in to hear him better. They had just parked in front of McDonalds and were getting ready to go in. He'd organized to meet Lucas and Sergio there for burgers so that he could congratulate them, and more importantly, figure out how to keep Sergio from mentioning the incident to his cousin or anyone else in the company. "You know this is a big deal. You shouldn't have left without making sure he wasn't in there," Scotty said to Lucas.

"We did," retorted Lucas. "Well, I did. He just disappeared. We called out for him a bunch of times and no one responded. I checked the entire place. Right, Serg? We checked everything," Lucas said as he looked over at Sergio in the passenger's seat. "Believe me, no one is there."

Scotty looked worried for a moment, but then realized he couldn't do anything and lightened up. "Okay, then. Well, maybe he just took off. Weird though–why would he do that? First he messes stuff up and gets hurt, then he dashes. I can't figure it out."

"You're telling me," Lucas said and then smiled a 'get out of jail free' smile. "Oh well, seems like everything is fine, and you guys pulled it off, so let's get some food. I'm starving."

"What a crazy day," Scotty said as he bumped fists with Lucas. The smell of the burgers permeated the warm night sky as they walked up to the doors and their stomachs growled. "You guys made it happen even though you lost your crew. Pretty cool."

Sergio chuckled for a moment, uncomfortable about what he knew and how the two of them were brushing it off as if nothing had happened. He wondered if they knew he'd paid the worker and told him to take off, but then he remembered how self-centered and oblivious guys like that were. In this, he folded his worry into calm.

"Lucas and I were thinking," Scotty started and then paused for a second, looking at Sergio "...you did so well today. You deserve some kind of promotion. I mean, you always work so hard and we're a team. We couldn't do it without you. I'm thinking I'll put you on as a foreman for the next job as long as everything goes smoothly for the rest of this one. How does that sound?" he asked Sergio as the unspoken promise sat in the air.

Sergio glanced at Scotty, then Lucas–they had made a pact and it was obvious. He needed the promotion, and they knew it, but he thought it hilarious that they seemed to think he was stupid enough to not recognize the bribe. Regardless, he was barely making it financially so he realized he would probably have to comply. For a moment he considered what that would mean. He'd get a car, make more money, which meant that he would be able to afford to send his daughter to preschool, and a whole lot of things would get better for him if he just shut up and kept his head down.

"Sounds good," he said and looked them straight in the

eye. "I'd really like the opportunity to lead a crew." With this, Scotty high fived him and smiled.

"Good then. Let's make sure things go well tomorrow, and I'll see what I can do to get you that position. I'm sure it will be a cinch."

8:16 p.m.

The air thinned as the front bell jingled and three men strolled in. They smelled like sweat. One of them was whistling softly, which immediately made Leona feel uneasy.

Leona looked at Esmeralda and she glanced back at her knowingly. The men had the kind of air all women know about; entitled and unnecessarily confident, or maybe it's aggressive. What's the difference? Trouble always whistles before it screams.

They were talking loudly, and to Leona, they seemed to be surveying the place to determine where they wanted to stake their claim. Her chest began to tighten as the men on horses from earlier that day resurfaced and the man at the bus stop reached out to grab her again. The confidence she'd been building gained fell to the wayside.

Esmeralda stood flush beside her and grasped her hand. Suddenly neither of them were themselves.

"What do you guys want?" the taller brunette asked his friends as they made their way up to the counter. Heavy footsteps echoed in Leona's ears as the image of yellow doors flashed before her eyes. She thought back to the dirty magenta rug she'd seen on the side of the road earlier.

What is happening? She thought as she tried to catch her breath. *I'm okay. I'm okay.* She told herself but her world rocked itself off of its axis.

The men's gaze crawled: Leona, Esmeralda, the empty tables. They seemed hungry, and she suddenly wanted to run off. She steadied herself.

The blonde eyed Leona and without hesitation said, "I see something I want." At this he placed his thumb into his jean pocket and wiggled it a bit which made his key jingle. He was a tall red-faced, muscular man with light blond curly hair and the stench of a malnourished animal. He looked like he'd been working on some kind of construction site because his clothes were filthy and a bit torn. His eyes cut into Leona as she tried to become invisible.

"Yeah, okay. Ha ha..." the dark haired man said to Lucas and wiped his mustache, "...but on the menu. What do you want?" he continued. The last man looked on, noticeably annoyed by the inappropriate innuendos of his coworkers. He stayed silent and tried to distance himself.

As they stood before her, Leona began to realize that she somehow knew the blonde. The memory sat like a bandit with a switchblade. It was there and breathing freely, just eyeing her, while she looked around to see if she could escape. She breathed in deeply and counted to six, then released her breath with the same timing. She had to stay calm. She had to be strong. It was all she knew to do.

Esmeralda suddenly grabbed her arm. She had let go but then shocked Leona by clasping onto her arm again. "Um... I'm going to take a break," she spit out in a hasty manner and rushed to the back. It was extremely out of character as Esmeralda had a strong demeanor and always stood tall despite her small stature.

"Are you okay?" Leona asked, turning around and ignoring the customers. "Do you need help?"

"No, no...I'm okay," Esmeralda lied as she rushed away.

The men at the counter seemed to laugh at this display of emotion.

How bad would it be if I just walked off? she thought. *I should be able to defend myself.*

She contemplated the prospect. While Esmeralda was in distress (most likely triggered by the harassment) the perverts walked freely. It sickened her and her steel heart pound for all of the women who had to deal with these kinds of men, including herself.

Anger rose in her as she peered at the blonde man. She didn't like it but she could feel hate boiling inside her. *What would happen if I punched him directly in the face? Maybe that would shut him up,* she thought. With this, her world began to spin and she held onto the counter.

(The Rug Shop, 2007)

Leona's family had only been in Los Angeles for only a few months when the glass shattered. She was fourteen at the time and felt like a tiny ant far away from its loving hilltop community after her recent move to the city. Nothing was familiar. Because of this she found herself reluctant to brave the lonely streets alone, even during the daytime. She was used to a much smaller town and safer neighborhoods. The streets should have been safe where she lived—everyone should be able to walk around without concern—but they weren't. Jolie, her newly minted best friend, had lived in the city for most of her life and knew where to turn—which routes to avoid—so Leona tried to stick by her side as much as possible.

She and Jolie had been walking home from Santee together for over a month, but on this particular cataclysmic day, Jolie had broken off from their path early so that she could hang out with her boyfriend before her mom got home. Jolie's mom's strict rules kept her on the hunt for privacy. After she left her, Leona's stomach began to ache. She wasn't hungry; she was nervous and rightfully so. Something was off, and she knew it, but because she was always afraid in the city, she had learned to ignore her intuition. On this day, and most days, she forced herself to move forward against her body's warnings.

A few minutes after walking solo, she heard men behind her, whistling and humming in the way all women know to be afraid of. Change was jingling in their pockets as they made their way to wherever they were going, and they were talking loudly like they owned the streets, moving with the confidence of leopards on the hunt. She didn't want to be the rabbit they would feed upon, but soon became aware of their intentions.

She turned the corner and hoped they didn't notice. She wanted to be invisible, so she visualized a force field around herself, protecting her soft flesh from greedy hands. This was no place for a lone girl and she knew it. She and Jolie had been approached multiple times in the last few months while walking home, and it was hard enough to ward them off as a pair, but something about Jolie's demeanor always seemed to scare the guys. Maybe she looked like she would yell? Leona never knew why, but she knew *she* appeared as an outsider and this brought unwanted attention. She wasn't sure if it was the way she walked or her darting eyes, but what she did know was that she was meat and they were hungry.

Leona breathed heavily as she felt the men inched behind her. They were a few feet away—maybe ten? She wasn't sure, but it was close enough that the hair on her neck stood on alert.

I am safe, she said to herself, trying to slow her breathing. *Act like you know what you're doing.* Murmuring fiction to herself was the only way she could calm her raging heart, so she repeated the lie. *I am invisible. I am safe. I am strong. This will be fine.*

To try to lose them, she moved faster, darting left into an alley and then right into another one, twisting as she willed them off and tried to look inconspicuous. As she sped up, however, so did they, however—coyotes on the scent. They seemed to laugh about the chase. They could taste her fear, and she could smell their intentions.

A yellow door on the side of a building beckoned to her, making its case as a possible escape, so she thrust it open. Unfortunately, it was an old rug shop and it led to nothing but a desolate room. Droves of rugs hung from the ceiling. Turkish. Armenian. Persian. The colors engulfed her and flooded her senses, and she slammed the door shut. *Maybe she could hide?*

They surrounded her within minutes.

I'm not afraid. There's nothing to fear.

"Hey little princess, where are you going? You're not scared, are you?" one of them said as he moved in towards her. He had a raspy voice and looked to be in his early twenties. He seemed like a loner to the world, but comfortable in this space of domination.

She was an injured wolf. Hungry mountain lions circling, about to pounce.

We see you.

Minutes passed and her head became hollow as her breathing swallowed. *What was happening?* The room began to spin. Her body's response was the exact opposite of what she wanted. She wanted to be steady and strong.

The rabbit had been caught.

"You want this," said a blond man in his early twenties, his hazy blue eyes biting into her. His crackling voice gave the impression that he was younger, either a late bloomer to puberty or a recent graduate.

To them, she was a plaything—a doll made of plastic.

He went in for the kill, laughing as he loosened his pants. Leona backed away from him, tripping over herself midstep. He grabbed her around the waist and pulled her jeans down, scrapping her roughly in the process.

This isn't happening. No one would really be this horrible.

"These ones are always the funniest," he said as he sunk into her. "You'll see..."

One of the guys in the back of the crowd laughed. It was a game.

She grit her teeth as he sunk into her and her head became light, feeling as if it was floating above her body. She didn't quite know what was happening as she'd never been touched by a man before, let alone attacked by one.

In rage, the blond used her like he had a hundred scores to make even, pinning her over a chair as she pleaded for him to stop, but she was an empty vessel to fill. He was consumed with aggression. She willed herself to fight back, but she couldn't move at all. Instead, she found herself frozen, never speaking

Is he going to kill me? How will I get out of here?

Despite her screams, he didn't stop. He didn't hear her, as she had become a mere silhouette of a young woman.

The rugs hung in droves on the walls—east, west, north, south—and she tried to focus on them. A magenta one stood out to her. They were innocent bystanders. All corners of the world screamed out for her, and she felt the pain of the past flowing into her. So many women had suffered her fate. So many sisters, mothers, nieces, and aunts called to her.

Stop.

At some point, another man took the first one's place and the pain continued. They were interchangeable—twins in rage, monsters in force. His course voice punctured her ears, and an old musty smell—the byproduct of blazing hot days and ancient textiles—filled her nostrils. She focused her attention on the shaggy reds, thin browns, and deep blood-like magentas in the rugs that were accented by sharp blues of the purest ocean, which allowed her to somewhat remove herself from her body. All of it was filtered through blurred vision as she gasped in pain.

With her cheek pushed up against the dusty old leather chair, the last guy took his turn with her. He seemed to be in his twenties as well, but was more reluctant than the blonde and the Russian. When they were done, they smoked a joint calmly and laughed in their accomplishment as she lay dying. An afternoon's work.

But she was hollow—skin and bones, no beating heart, no ability to reason. Her prayers fell on the cement floor with no god to save her.

Am I still alive? Will I die? Is anything real?

She rolled over and collapsed on the couch to rest, trying to be invisible. She was afraid any movement would start the attack over again. It seemed they hung around for hours afterwards as she wanted her flesh, having been ripped raw, burned with fire. The rug shop shrunk as did her head.

How long had it been? *Ten minutes? Two hours?* Eventually they left, and in an instant she found herself in a fierce panic, alone, shaking, and crying. She had to figure out how to pull herself back together so that she could get home.

Her limbs were numb, and at some point, she pulled the skinny jeans her mom had bought her during their "back to school shopping" up and stumbled out into the alleyway, half-alert, with tears running down her face. She walked home as a ghost.

Everywhere she looked, the world dripped with blood.

When she finally got there, her mom called out, but she walked past her, ghostlike, and got straight into the shower. It was like she was returning from her own funeral, as she ripped her clothes off angrily and let the hot water run down her naked body. She couldn't do anything to escape the feel of their hands, their bodies pushed against her. She couldn't wash their filth off. Welts rose on her skin from the excessive scrubbing as she screamed into the water. She got out and sank deeply into her sheets, never before feeling so alone.

Numb, she lay trembling until she passed out from exhaustion. Later that night, she woke up in a fever, and after she calmed herself down, she began to wonder at what point a boy decides to become a rapist.

She vowed to never tell anyone. What she didn't know then was that rape is a hungry virus that lives inside a person forever. It turns a healthy nervous system into writhing worms.

And this is why Leona hasn't been okay. She's not walking around all light and fluttery like so many of her peers. She should be able to be free in her early twenties before the throes of life are thrust upon her, but she has been heavy for years.

When she told me about the rape years after it happened, I could not believe she had held it in for so long. I so wish she would have let it out earlier. Maybe it wouldn't have made her so fraught with inner turmoil. But I shouldn't wish anything different. She did what she could do. No one should have to deal with this violence and if they do, we should never say they should have reacted differently. That's not fair. There's no playbook for this. It doesn't matter that it's common. And think about it, why is *this* common? What a mess.

And so many of us hold this trauma as if it's some type of wicked secret that we've brought upon ourselves, as if we asked for it.

I wish I could have helped. I could have been there for her or got her to therapy back then. I hate to know that she had suffered in silence for so many years. I feel that I was part of the problem for not recognizing that something was wrong. My own daughter, Cecilia, had those darkened eyes. I should have noticed the change. I should have, but I didn't.

She thinks I'm so strong, but I didn't even notice her suffering.

9:13 p.m.

Leona tried to push her unsteady feeling to the back of her mind as she took a deep breath and faced the man.

"I'll have a Spicy Crispy Chicken Sandwich with two orders of fries. I'm hungry," he said with an offending stare. "You got that, sweetie?"

I'll show you where to put that "sweetie," she thought and imagined smacking him square in the face. As violence rose in her, she pushed it away. *I'm a pacifist.* She'd grown so much that day and she wasn't going to let it fall away so easily.

"Anything else?" She asked the man as she felt her heart thumping. It was throwing itself against the walls of her body with anxious fists: one for a gut punch and another for a hand to the air. She decided she would stare this man straight in the eye and meet him where he was. He was trying to make her uncomfortable; she'd do the same.

"No, I'm good," he said as he handed her his credit card. He held his eyes to hers and looked to be undressing her as he looked down to her chest. She felt invaded.

The blond, who had made her stomach turn earlier,

stepped up to the counter, and she felt the anxious dizziness creeping in. She breathed in and slowly let it out.

"You look familiar," he said. She felt her stomach knot up, realizing that she'd thought the same thing minutes before. *How did she know him?* Her vision blurred.

"What can I get you?" she asked, trying not to meet his gaze. She didn't know if she could handle it. If she met eyes, she might turn into something. At this point, she wasn't sure what that would be.

Bells tolled in the distance and a fire truck blazed down the street.

"Hmmm...not sure. You don't recognize me?" he asked as his face broke into a wry smile, white incisors popping out like a wolf's bite.

"What do you want?" she interrupted him in an apathetic tone.

Just ignore him, she thought. *Don't let him in at all.*

He gazed at her, "I'll have the juiciest burger you've got. I like it really juicy. You know what I mean."

"Okay, Double Quarter Pounder it is," she said as she avoided him.

He extended his credit card, and in doing so held onto it a bit too long for her comfort before releasing it to her fingers. For a moment she fell into the fear. The world turned and she held onto the counter. After what seemed like forever, his payment went through and she handed the card back to him.

"I'll call your number when it's ready."

"I can't wait," he said.

"Well, you'll have to," she fired back. He looked at her for a moment, surprised.

"You need to be more professional," he shot back, seeming to want to say more but then he turned to the man next to him. "It's all you, Serg. Be careful with this one."

Rage and violence welled up inside of her as her belly

growled fiercely, and she thought of all of the ways she should put him in his place. The ebb and flow of natural anger and forced calm continued. The man walked over to meet his friends at the table. The two of them made themselves comfortable with their feet up on the chairs. They seemed to be used to doing whatever they pleased.

The last man approached and placed his order. She expected the same behavior, but to her surprise he wasn't like them. His curly dark hair framed his face in a boyish way and he smiled a genuine smile as he tried to make light of what had just happened.

"Sorry about those guys," he said. "Stuck in the old days, I guess."

Without intending to, Leona interrupted him with a forced laugh. "Oh, is that what it is? They seem like harassers, not the 'oops, I'm accidentally being inappropriate' types."

"Oh, well yeah, maybe," he seemed shocked by her straight forward demeanor. "Anyways, I have kids. Two girls. If anyone ever treated them like that, I'll..." He continued as he cleared his throat and took his wallet out. "Anyways, thanks. You deserve to make a lot more for having to deal with people like them."

"No amount of money would be worth it," she responded, while in disbelief that she had actually said it aloud. Her silence was no longer stuck in her chest. It seemed to have sprung free and was running wildly.

"Well, next time, just ignore them," he said. "They'll leave you alone if they don't see that it upsets you. I'm with these guys all day, unfortunately, and I see how they are. They're trying to get a rise out of people."

Leona looked up at him. "Is that what I should do, ignore them? Does ignoring things really work?" she asked, wondering if he could sense her sarcasm. She wanted to explain that ignoring the harassment wouldn't make things change— that it was the reason people still acted this way. Instead, she said, "Your order will be up in a minute," and looked away.

He nodded and said, "True, I guess it doesn't. Anyways, sorry about them."

With this, he walked over to meet his coworkers who were chatting and laughing, seemingly oblivious to everything around them, including the conversation he'd just had with Leona.

Esmeralda walked back up and called the number that was up. The blonde man walked up to grab it and began staring at Leona once again. "Wow, that was fast. You must have done me a favor," he said.

"Nope," Esmeralda answered and promptly handed him his food without looking at him.

"Are you okay?," Leona asked as she leaned towards her. "What happened back there?"

"I don't know...I was fine and then I just felt like throwing up, like everything I hate in the world was coming to a head all at once in that man's face. He didn't even have to do anything. Sometimes I think it's all just too much. All of this, it's too much."

"I feel you. And you were right, they were perverts," she said.

Esmeralda closed her eyes and Leona gave her a hug. "I knew it. It's strange how our bodies react before our mind does, isn't it. I felt it as soon as they walked in."

"Yeah, it is. We know who is out to get us. That's why we need to stick together and fight back."

" Fight back physically?"

"Maybe," she said in a pause, while considering.

"We'd never win."

"You never know," Leona responded.

"I think I do, Leona. I think we both know how that ends."

Leona had always thought Esmeralda had been raped and in this moment she saw she was right. There's a certain unspoken camaraderie women have when they meet someone else who has gone through their pain. It's as if they wear a badge. It's a badge of horror.

Across the restaurant, the man looked over at Leona again and she clenched her jaw. *Where did she know him from?* Her stomach knotted.

Esmeralda noticed and asked, "You okay?"

"Yeah, I'm fine," she said. It was a decision to be okay, and in it she felt as brave as the sun.

Off to College

I don't want to be brave; I want to be free.

* * *

In August of 2021, a 17 year old female student was allegedly raped by a 19 year old male member of the Fiji (Phi Gamma Delta) fraternity at a party on the campus of University of Nebraska-Lincoln. After the alleged assault, the university temporarily shut down the fraternity while it investigated the case but did not suspend it indefinitely. The fraternity had been suspended before when some of its members were charged with sexual harassment during a women's march on campus. It has a history of misconduct.

Many students believed that the university leadership was acting too slowly and took to the streets to protest the lack of action on the university's part. They wanted the university to be proactive in their approach and respond with rape counseling for the victim and consequences for the perpetrator. Currently, universities around the country are experiencing a dramatic increase in protests on campus regarding sexual assault and harassment. Much of this is due to a sharp increase in reporting by the victims and more awareness of assault and harassment on social media platforms. Still, rape on college campuses is common. As of 2020, 26.4% of female undergraduates are raped (by force or incapacitation) and many of the assaults happen within the first few months of their college experience.

9:16 p.m.

"I'm gonna step out for a second," Sergio said as he motioned to Lucas. "If you could grab my food that would be great."

"Okay, can't wait to tell your wife about the promo?" Scotty said in a laugh. "I get it. She's going to be excited. Maybe you'll get some tonight, huh?" he said with a wink.

Sergio cleared his throat, disgusted. He wanted to unload on them, both of them, but the money they needed was in clear sight, so he kept quiet. He saw a future for his girls and that had to be the focus.

His wife didn't pick up so he left a voice message. It was late, so she was probably putting the kids to bed. He could see her now, in her black nightshirt, with her long dark hair tangled up in a bun while she read the girls' The *Giving Tree*. Every night they giggled and snuggled up to her. He wanted nothing more than to be there, by her side, as she read and sang to them.

Sweetie, I'm done now and grabbing dinner. Don't wait up.

We'll be late. He doesn't have a family so you know how that goes. Good news! I got a raise. It's kind of complicated, and we'll see if these guys follow through, but it seems like they might. Things should be better for us from now on. I think I might even get a truck. Who knows? We shouldn't get our hopes up. Also, don't worry, I gave that worker who got hurt a wad of cash and told him to take off before something worse happened. These guys are assholes, but you already knew that. Anyways, love you to the moon and back. I'll make sure to hug you when I crawl into bed next to you later though. Say goodnight to my sweet peas.

When he walked back into the bright lights, Lucas and Scotty were stuffing their faces with fries. He sat down and ate slowly, thinking about how things had taken a turn. Scotty stopped for a second and asked, "Did you see the tits on the girl at the counter?"

"Yes, sir," Lucas responded and the two of them laughed.

Sergio grunted. He was disgusted by the way they interacted and treated others. For a moment, he considered telling them off again. *They are pigs,* he thought. *I can't work with these guys.*

But then he noticed the writing on the wall, and it was in bold lettering.

9:36 p.m.

A woman entered McDonald's with a UCLA sweatshirt on, and it reminded Leona to check her email.

"I'm going on a quick break, okay? Just let Marcus know when he comes over. I'm waiting to find out about school, and I want to see if I got in." Leona said as Esmeralda opened her eyes wide in anticipation.

"You'll get in. You're the smartest person I know," she replied. "If you don't get in, no one should."

"Thanks, girl. My grades are solid, but so much of it is luck."

"I guess you're right," Esmeralda replied, smiling as she helped herself to a spoonful of soft serve. Leona copied her quickly, also grabbing a handful of fries before ducking out. The ice cream melted slowly on her tongue, soothing her with sweetness, and the fries complemented it well, answering with a salty tang. She checked her phone for the long-awaited email.

A message with UCLA was in the title, but when she pressed on it. There was no text.

Well, that isn't helpful, she thought, making a mental note to email admissions about it.

She looked around, letting herself relax for a moment. She took it all in. The day had been long and her breaks had been littered with chaos, just like the room she sat in. It seemed her coworkers hadn't cared enough to throw out their trash, and the table was messy, with ketchup, salt, and dirty napkins covering the top. She pushed it aside to make room for her elbows, but someone's napkin was stuck to the bottom of the basket. It was ripped in half, which seemed fitting. The fries she had grabbed for her dinner were piping hot, and she reveled in the savory taste, allowing each potato strip to melt on her tongue as she bit into it. She appreciated this tiny thing and meditated on it for a moment. She thought back to what she'd just said with Esmeralda. *Maybe we could win*, she thought. *Maybe if we fought back, if we all did, every time, things would change.* The idea washed over her and the fleeting but strong feeling of possibility sat in her for a moment. She leaned into the power, and for a moment she felt as if peace had descended upon her.

Everything is going to be okay, she thought. *It will all work out.*

But will it? It's so easy to imagine a better world, one in which people respect each other's right to privacy and space, their right to exist in their own way and have control of their own bodies, but it's another thing to make it happen. How many activists have fought their entire lives for this cause only to die with legislation or societal norms in a similar spot?

I know I sound cynical, but after I stopped singing and settled into the habit of reading books about civil rights and feminism, I noticed how little has changed. Maybe Leona knows something I don't. Maybe the younger generations will be the ones who finally put an end to all of this torment. Maybe they'll have the awakening and the skills to make it happen. Maybe this will be the tipping point. I doubt it, but there's always a chance.

When I think of this, I think about the old speech "Are Women Persons?" from Susan B. Anthony. She changed everything with logic and by putting her body on the line. I'm sure that no one expected her to do this. Although her argument was reasonable, I'm sure many just assumed that she would be dismissed. I mean, she was initially, but eventually she got through to them once she found herself in court defending her right to vote. Should a person have to go this far? Shouldn't each person have inherent rights?

Okay, okay, I'm on a tangent. There's no point in getting all wrapped up in a philosophical debate and passing on my existential crisis to you.

Leona's particular McDonald's was open 24 hours a day, but as a staff they had to act like they were closing, and check off the lists, so they could make sure to get everything done before the graveyard shift came in. The floors were sticky and the place was aging, in need of some serious remodeling, but no one seemed to really notice. It would probably be that way until it shut its doors one day.

Marcus glared at Leona as she walked out of the break room.

"I didn't do anything. You know I'll get it all done," she said to him as he turned the corner to the back of the house. He huffed and kept walking. He seemed to be exhausted by the night.

Leona went back up to the front, seeing the men who'd disturbed her throw their scraps into the trash and saunter out just as casually as they had come in. She threw a silent spell at them and cursed their steps.

"Goodbye Fuckers," she remarked under her breath and imagined them vanishing into thin air. She wouldn't cause them pain, but she would do something that would make them regret their actions and think again next time. What would that be? If only she had so much power.

Esmeralda heard her and joined in. "Yeah, get the fuck out and don't come back," she said.

Just then, as if he had heard them, the blond turned back and looked straight at Leona, thrusting her into straight panic. She grimaced, felt instantly sick, and had the urge to flip him off, but didn't, knowing he would probably like it. Instead she just glared back at him, feigning strength.

Her world spun for just a second.

He doesn't deserve an ounce of my energy, she thought. *Absolutely nothing.*

9:58 p.m.

"That girl was ripe," Lucas said as he settled into the seat of his truck, after saying goodbye to Scotty, and looked back through the window of McDonald's to soak Leona in. "She was acting all innocent, but she knows me. We used to fuck."

'I doubt that," Sergio said, as he looked over and laughed. From his perspective there wasn't an ounce of truth in it. Lucas was ripe with insecurity, and therefore, prone to lying. From what he could tell Leona looked much younger than Lucas, about ten years roughly, and she'd been so upset by them. *They didn't seem to know each other at all, and why would she fake it if she did?* Something about it didn't make sense. He was learning it was best to keep quiet with Lucas. Then he wouldn't have to hear more.

Sergio looked out the window at the bright night sky and across the street where a 24 hours a day laundromat was buzzing with people; he wished he was there. He wanted to be anywhere but with Lucas.

"No, we did. I still remember. She was a feisty one."

Sergio continued to look away, trying to send subtle hints

that he'd had enough, and then he looked ahead and said, "Let's get going. My wife and kids are waiting for me."

Lucas grunted in irritation. It was obvious he wanted to finish the story. "But look how good she looks," he said, intent on staring at Leona. "I just want to look at her all night. I deserve something like that at the end of a hard day."

"Well, maybe you shouldn't have fucked it up with her then," Sergio shot back, failing to keep his cool. "You're acting like some type of pervert. You think women like that? Let's go. I am exhausted."

"Sorry, old man, I forgot it's past your bedtime," Lucas said as he turned on the engine. "Got to get you home to your mama."

"Fuck you," Sergio said, and before he could think of his actions, or the consequences that would come from them, he turned to Lucas and spit in his face. "You're an asshole, you know. A pathetic loser. A liar. A horrible person. The way you treated that guy on the jobsite earlier was pitiful. I know it was your fault–you never turned the gas off. I was with you! And you just harassed the hell out of that woman who you say you dated. I think you're a lying piece of shit."

In full force and without warning, Lucas headbutted Sergio and spit at him. "Get out. How dare you talk to me that way. After everything I've done for you. Who do you think you are? I never should have picked you up, you dirty Mexican."

Sergio cupped his head in pain, feeling the demons swell up inside of him as he considered retaliation. Lucas definitely deserved it. In his younger years, Sergio used to be a boxer and knew he could pound Lucas to a pulp. He would never know what hit him. Instead, he looked Lucas straight in the eyes and decided he wasn't worth it. "I hope you get what's coming to you. One day it will happen. Take my word for it," he said, and with this, he grabbed his bag and got out of the car.

"You're a pussy, a fucking loser," Lucas yelled at him as he screeched off in the Los Angeles night.

The pain in Sergio's head was fierce, but he was proud he had stood up for himself, the worker, and the woman. His family flashed in front of his eyes–there would be birthdays and sunsets for years to come and no amount of satisfaction would be worth the problems that might have come from retaliation.

He was free.

10:21 p.m.

"Any news about UCLA?" Esmeralda asked.

"Nah, nothing," Leona answered. "Carlos didn't get in, so I don't even know if I care as much now. I can't imagine going without him."

"Girl, you can't let that get to you. He's awesome, but this is your future. You've got to go if you get in."

"Yeah, well he's my future too..." she shot back. "And what do you know? You're only in high school," she continued.

"Oh, sorry...didn't know that your boyfriend is your future."

"Shut up," Leona said, realizing how stupid it sounded. "No, you're right...we'll make it through, I guess. I shouldn't doubt things so much."

"Exactly," she answered. "That's my Leona, being the strong bitch you are. You aren't dependent on no man."

"Damn straight," Leona said, only half believing it. "But he is a good one though. You've got to keep the good ones."

. . .

The bell sounded at the front and the elderly woman from the bus earlier walked in with a colorful collection of plastic bags in tow and a giant bohemian blanket decorated with a Santa Fe design draped over her arm. She had a way of swooping in, as if flying rather than walking, and this movement made her seem magical. She was dirty but she still seemed entreating for some reason, almost ancient.

"Bruja is here," Esmeralda whispered, laughing slightly as she leaned towards Leona. They giggled like children as they watched the elderly woman with tangled gray hair and a stained sage dress sauntered in. She was always unkempt and slightly frightening.

"I saw her on the bus earlier," Leona whispered to Esmeralda... "but she wouldn't look at me as usual. I'm not sure if she saw me at all. She is such a strange lady."

"I'll go get her some water. I'm sure she's thirsty," Esmeralda said. They often contemplated whether she was someone's grandmother, mother, or daughter, and her long gray locks reminded them that they would look that way one day.

"She looks like she's had a rough day," Leona responded as she refilled the sticky ketchup dispensers again, the odor of expired ketchup reaching for her nostrils, making her feel slightly nauseous. "...more difficult than usual at least."

To them, Bruja seemed to be a sweet yet lost older woman who had been forgotten. It looked as if she'd been on her own for at least a decade or so. Most of her teeth were missing, her body was misshapen, and her eyes had distinct crows feet, probably from squinting in the morning sun. From what they knew, she wandered around and took buses most of the day, not seeming to stay in one place for long. Bruja wore wild recycled clothes, but somehow carried the fresh smell of the trees rather than a stench. Tonight she had on a long black shawl and it was flung over her shoulders despite the heat of the day.

Much to their dismay, instead of going to a table in the back to set her stuff down as usual and then heading to the restroom, she walked straight up to them. As she approached, she looked Leona deep in the eyes and suddenly she was in a trance. It frightened her for a moment. Then, without warning, Bruja lifted her hand up and extended Atzi's swallow key out to her. The gold sparkled in the fluorescent lighting.

"What? No way!" Leona screamed as she took it from the woman's cupped hand. "How did you find this? And how did you know it was mine?"

Bruja stared at her and said, "I asked it, and it told me." With this, she smiled a mostly toothless grin and stepped back a bit.

"But how...?" Leona asked in surprise.

Esmeralda and Leona looked at each other in disbelief, not understanding what the elderly woman was talking about. Then, a silent door opened between Leona and the woman as she realized that Bruja was more than who she seemed to be. She was some type of enchantress it seemed, not one of darkness and evil. She glowed with energy and an age-old wisdom that rang vaguely familiar.

"If you listen, truly listen to things," Bruja continued, pushing her long gray hair back behind her shoulder on the right side to show her ear and mimic listening. "...they will tell you where they belong. I found this on the bus, and when I held it up, the sun shone through it. I could see that it had been in your family for ages, and I knew it was important to you. You see, I have been watching you."

"What do you mean?" Leona asked, suddenly afraid. "I see you most days but you never look at me."

"I don't look at you when you're looking," she answered. "I pay attention to you when you're distracted, which you often are. That way it's easier for me to see who you really are. Because I do this, I can see that you are one hell of a woman. You work so hard and have so much strength."

"Oh, well thank you. I have to say it makes me a little bit nervous you're watching me, but I appreciate the compliment. I can't believe I have Atzi's key back," she said with a nervous laugh and jumped a bit in place. The excitement was overwhelming. Her heart beat quickly with adrenaline. She wanted to yell at the top of her lungs with joy. "You have no idea how much this means to me."

"I'm so glad to deliver the gift to you," Bruja said. "You deserve it."

"Well, thank you so much!" Leona said. "This holds everything I care about," she said as she admired the swallow on the head of the key and traced it with her fingertip like she'd done so hundreds of times before.

Bruja smiled again. Showing a cavernous mouth that looked like that of a baby's, soft and innocent.

"The key doesn't hold your power, you know? It's a symbol," Bruja continued, sounding simple and practical. Mysticism seemed to be the furthest thing from the woman's mind. "It only sings because you have given it a voice."

"Well, it seems to have power to me," Leona responded. "It holds the hope of a better future because that's what it did for my family. My great grandmother, Atzi, used it to heal people back in Mexico and then my grandmother, Xochitl, gave it to me before she died. It's all I have from her. It's my everything."

"That's beautiful," Bruja said. "...but I want you to know that you're strong without it. You have your own fire. It sits in your belly. All of us have this, but many of us ignore it."

"Hmmm, I guess so..." Leona asked, contemplating the face of the woman who seemed to know so much. She was still in shock about the return of this prized possession and confused about how Bruja knew it was hers. Moreover, it seemed that this woman she'd dismissed as homeless for years now was quite the wise elder. She felt bad that she'd expected Bruja to be mentally ill or a selective mute. It was a lesson in assumptions. "Who are you?" Leona muttered as she peered into the woman's deep eyes.

"Well, it's complicated," she said. "My story is old, like that of a tree with its twisting and prodding roots, but it's also new, like the first moment a fresh born lamb breathes in air. It's a circle actually. Most things go around and around, like the turning of the earth or the ebbing of the tide."

"Do you have a minute to explain?" Leona asked. "I have so many questions. You're so interesting, and we know so little. And you returned the most important thing to me. I'd love to understand you."

Esmeralda placed her arm around Leona's shoulder and listened with her. She seemed to be just as intrigued by Bruja's transformation as Leona was.

"Okay, girls, but first, I need to use the restroom. It's been a longer day than you can imagine. I've been up since sunrise."

"Of course," Leona said. "We'll be right here waiting for you.

As the woman turned to use the restroom, Esmeralda faced Leona. She seemed to be glowing. "Maybe we had her all wrong," she said. "Seems she's more of an angel than a witch."

"Most definitely. I didn't even know she could talk, let alone say anything important."

"Just goes to show...some of life's best things are right in front of our face."

"I still can't believe I got this back," Leona said once more, holding it in her palm and letting the gold chain fall down around her fingers. "It means everything to me."

"You do know that she's right, don't you?" Esmeralda asked Leona. "You grew on your own today. Didn't you notice how strong you were? You stood up for that little lost girl and you stayed fierce with those perverts. And the key was gone at that point. You thought you'd never see it again, so it wasn't the key that had the power. Something has changed in you. You're not usually this bold."

"Yes, I am," she fought back as Esmeralda looked sideways at her. She knew it was a lie.

"No, honey, you're not. Not even close."

* * *

As Bruja walked back up, Leona noticed that she looked different. Something seemed to have shifted. Her walk was a bit lighter and her hair seemed to regain some of its dark sheen rather than looking gray as it did before.

"So...where was I?" she asked, as she settled into a booth and put her hands on the table as if to begin a long story.

"Well, I guess the first question is who are you and why have you been hiding from us this entire time?" Leona asked as she looked Bruja deep in the eyes. "You're so cool."

"You weren't ready for this," she answered.

"Ready for what?" Leona prompted.

"I guess to know what's coming towards you and do something about it," Bruja said as she handed her a book. It was tattered and worn but Leona recognized it immediately. It was *Handmaid's Tale* by Margaret Atwood.

"My grandmother, Xochitl, had that and she talked about it all the time. It was like a bible for her," Leona said. "She always said we had to be careful or we could end up like the women in Gilead. She said we had to protect our rights, even the tiny ones, to prevent this from happening. I never read it though. Not sure why."

"Your grandmother, huh? She sounds like a really cool lady," Bruja said with a wrinkled brow and an odd look on her face. There was something there, but Leona couldn't figure it out.

Esmeralda took the book from Leona and flipped through it. "I've heard of this. My English teacher talked about it, but I never read it either."

"Well, it's something you should both get into. I used to be an activist when I was younger and this book was one of the things that prompted me, or rather scared me, into action. The idea that the old traditional ways could return or maybe even get worse for women, made me move out of my comfort zone and start fighting for our rights and ideals," Bruja said as she stared at her palms.

Leona noticed a small feather tattooed on her inner forearm was black toned and shaded with intricate detail. Leona sat in daydream about what it could mean while Bruja continued on with her story. She noticed she had missed a huge chunk of what Bruja had said while she was daydreaming.

"...and everything changed, not for the worse, but the fight had just shifted. We had new things to advocate for. That was before the transformation, but like I said, it is a circle so I know it will come back around and be even better as you guys work towards what it could be. It's about passing the knowledge and energy forward and inspiring the next generation to fight for what we worked so hard to gain."

"Wait, what happened?" Leona asked. "How did things change? What are you talking about?"

"Haven't you been paying attention, my sweet girl?" Bruja asked, as she laughed a bit and moved her long dress over to one side of her body, exposing a long dark leg that was adorned with hundreds of colorful tattooed flowers.

"Yes, but I'm still in a daze. Sorry, this is all so surprising," Leona said.

"I hate to bother you while you're having what seems to be a great chat, but we have work to do," Marcus interrupted Leona mid-sentence as he walked over and then looked over to smile at Bruja.

They all looked up at him, having not seen him approaching, and shuffled in their seats. "Okay," Leona said, "We'll just be a minute...Bruja...oops...I mean this kind woman...we never should have called you that...found my family's heirloom, this key," she said as she held up the swallows key, "...she brought it back to me. I dropped it earlier when I fell on the bus. I'm so happy. We just need a minute, please."

"Just a few minutes. We have a ton of work to do," he said. "Did you thank her?"

"Yes, of course!" Leona said.

"No, I mean truly thank her, like by getting her some food?"

"No," Leona said as she gasped. She couldn't believe she hadn't thought of that. Bruja was unhoused and probably starving. She turned towards the woman. "Are you hungry? Would you like my meal?" Leona asked. "I'd be more than happy to give my shift leaders meal."

"That's okay, my dear. I have plenty. I have everything I need and more." At this, Leona and Esmeralda looked at each other in confusion.

She did? Leona thought. *Had they been completely wrong about her?*

Bruja continued. "I came to give you the key and the book. Everything else is in its place. I have what I need and now, so do you," Bruja answered. She held a foreign look in her eyes as if she had already left and then she began to rise. "I better be going now, my sweet loves."

"No. please. We want to know more. We still don't know your story," Leona pleaded, as she motioned for her to stay and patted the plastic seat next to her.

"Yes, you do, sweetie. Think about it, you know my story. It's the same as yours. It's the same as your friend there," she said, motioning to Esmeralda. "It's the same as your aunt's, your grandmother's and your great grandmother's. We all have the same story. It just unfolds itself in different ways. It's my job to make sure you see this and keep the cycle moving so that the younger ones have a better time at it. I want to make sure you know your strength."

At this, she gathered her bags and bowed at them. "Remember, whatever happens, you are ready. Don't doubt yourself, even for a moment. I believe that you will know what to do."

"Wait, what do you mean?" Leona asked, in confusion. "Is something coming?"

As Bruja left she lifted a hand up and waved goodbye, but never turned to face them. They watched in awe of the strange woman.

"What in the world was that?" Leona asked Esmeralda. "Who is she?"

Esmeralda shrugged, "I have no idea, but I like her."

"And I just realized she said 'your aunt' to me. How would she know about my Aunt Cecila? She died years ago, but I never mentioned that. I am so spooked."

Esmeralda stood thinking about it for a moment, and then said, "I don't know. That's weird. She seemed to know a lot of shit she shouldn't know, but I hope we see her again. I need someone like that in my life. I already feel stronger." She stopped and turned to Leona. "I can't believe we called her a witch."

"Oh my god, I know," Leona responded. "We were so wrong."

What they didn't know was that her name wasn't Bruja, or anything resembling the traditional sense of the word. Her name is Tatiana and we've known each other since our mid-twenties when I first got to LA and was still singing. I think she was inspired by my story and how I ran away from my husband when I saw that he was becoming abusive. She had wanted to leave a dangerous lover at the time but found it difficult to actually do it. I think I gave her the push to make a move. It's one thing to know what you should do; it's an entirely different thing to do it. And although she was an outspoken advocate of women's rights, she was having a hard time putting her foot down when it came to her own life. So many of us deal with personal paradox. It's the mixed messages our society sends us–be accommodating and feminine, but also be strong and pave your own way. Which is it? Decide already. I guess the problem is that we were letting the men decide who we were instead of determining it ourselves, not to mention that being a woman looks different to everyone, so there's no variety in this.

Anyway, Tatiana found me and the kids, and we became instant friends. Tatiana, or Tati, as I called her, was very involved in activism and was the reason I learned so much about women's rights in the first place. I was a woman without an ideology and because of this I wasn't very powerful. I knew I believed in equal rights and freedom, for both myself and others, but I didn't know there were groups of people all over the country, or world for that matter, that were fighting for these causes. It seemed like a long slow fight, but

Tati showed me how to do it. Once I started learning, I fell in love with making things better. She's the reason I wrote all of my letters to the women in our family too. It was something she'd done for me and our friends. The magic started with her.

Unfortunately, I lost touch with her after Cecilia died. She had her own worries to deal with so I assumed that was why we stopped talking, but the truth of the matter was that she left us. Years passed and I didn't know what had happened to her until I got to this new place between life and death. Now the two of us are close again and it feels grand. You wouldn't believe how much we get to see each other. It's delightful.

Tati floats between worlds. For part of each day she's in ours and sits up here with us, trying to warn others of their paths and send energy out to those in"the trenches." The other half, she takes on a human form because we all know humans can't, or rather won't, take anything besides themselves seriously. They see us as cute or simple and push our trees aside as something to lean on or bulldoze.

* * *

The stockroom was bustling, everyone trying to get out before the 11pm turnover. As soon as she got back into work, her phone buzzed. It was a text from Jas. It had to be important. He never called.

Call me now.

In a matter of seconds, he texted her again. "It's about Papa."

At the thought of Xavier, Leona's heart rose and then sank. *Was he hurt? Or maybe worse, dead?* She braced herself for the bad news. She decided that she didn't care if she got in trouble and quickly dialed him. Some things were more important than following the rules.

Jas picked up.

"Hey, what's up?" she asked in a low tone, trying to skirt attention from her coworkers, knowing she'd already taken too many breaks. They walked around her in an irritated fashion; clearly it wasn't just Marcus who was frustrated with her. Marcus was up front, consumed with teaching a new worker to sweep properly, so she assumed she had a few minutes to spare.

"We found Dad."

"What?" she said with a gasp. "How?" Her heart was filled with butterflies, and a thousand questions flooded her mind, as she pictured her step-father. "What happened? Is he okay? Did you talk to him?"

"Yeah, for a few minutes. He seemed really shaken up. Apparently he's been in a detention center since last May, and they wouldn't let him make any calls. He somehow got put into solitary confinement because he was around when some type of scuffle happened, and they assumed he was part of it. They finally deported him after months of holding him. I think he's been beaten or something because he's not talking much, and he won't explain anything. It's like he's blocked everything out. I'm scared for him."

Anger welled up inside of her. Xavier, the man with the purest heart and the kindest of intentions shouldn't be treated that way. The desire to advocate for victims burned in her with a new urgency. She wanted to put a stop to this kind of thing.

Her rage turned to anxiety as a mixture of fear and empathy washed over her, realizing he might be irreparably damaged. "Where is he?" she asked. She had come to the conclusion that she'd never see him again a long time ago, and the fact that he was alive hit hard.

"He's with his sister in Guadalajara. I guess he just got there last night. She said he's been acting strange, like a ghost. I'm worried."

"Shit. I hope he's okay. I am so glad he's alive. So glad."

They sat in silence for a moment and took it in as their tears fell.

"How's my mom?" she asked through her sobs. "I'm surprised she didn't call me," she said as she remembered the missed call. "Oh wait, I think she did."

"She's a mess. You know how they were in that huge fight the morning before he was taken. We both know she didn't take it well. I'm not sure what she'll do with this, but so far she seems relieved."

Leona thought back to her mom, sitting in her pink robe and rocking in her ratty green chair. She shook her head to get the image out of her mind.

"How are you? Are you okay?" she asked Jas. She knew he was overjoyed to know his dad was alive, but shock is shock, so it would take a while to settle in.

He cleared his throat. "I'm so happy, but also weirded out, like I'm not sure if it's real. I keep calling him back, just to make sure he's really there. I was supposed to go into work tonight, but they'll have to do without me."

Marcus walked up and scowled at Leona. "What the?" he mouthed.

She interrupted and said, "We found my dad!" At this, he shook his head, not understanding the gravity of the situation.

He shrugged, "Okay..."

Leona smiled and returned to her conversation with Jas. "Do you think I could call him?"

"I don't see why not," he responded and then gave her the aunt's number. "He asked about you, so I'm sure he'll be happy if you reach out."

She hung up and dialed his number.

I can't believe he's alive, she thought as she listened to the ringing.

The seconds dragged on. There was a pause and then a

shuffle as if pages were turning. Xavier answered slowly and his voice crackled. "Bueno," Xavier said with stunted breathing, a slight cough releasing itself from captivity.

"Papa! It's Leona," she yelled. "I missed you so much. Jas said you're alive, you're out. I can't believe it!"

"Leo, my little bird. It's so good to hear your voice. How are you? I missed you! I'm so, so..." he said as he broke down crying. She could hear his voice cracking as he tried to formulate more words. It was unlike him to lose control.

"I love you, Dad," she said as she called him that for the first time. "I'm so happy to talk to you. We thought you were..."

"Don't say it, mija. Never say it," he said, hastily putting an end to her catastrophic thinking. "I'm alive, and I'm so sorry..."

"Sorry for what? You have nothing to be sorry for. I'm sorry this happened to you. Those animals," she responded, feeling a boil rise in her chest. *How could anyone hurt a person like him?* The image of crows stealing blue robin eggs out of a nest came to mind. For a moment, she felt violence creeping up inside of her and then reminded herself that she was a pacifist. Her thoughts had been creeping towards aggression all day.

"I'm sorry you guys didn't know where I was. I wanted to call you, but they kept me alone. I just got out and was sent home. Are you okay?" he explained.

"Yes, I'm fine but I'm so angry they did that to you. Everyone deserves to be able to talk to their family. I want to kill them."

"I know, but I'm okay now, Leo. I'm okay. Let's focus on that," Xavier's softness of spirit rose up again, and she remembered why she loved him so much. "I don't want you to hate. Remember all of those civil rights movements we've talked about? Well, none of that was done with violence or revenge. I want you to be peaceful, even in the face of injustice."

"Well, they didn't have to treat you that way. It's not fair," she continued, having a difficult time calming herself down. "It's one thing to take someone and keep them locked up, but it's another to isolate them. That's animalistic."

"Okay, true, but let's not focus on that. Let's focus on love and the future. I love you, and I'm glad we get to talk. Hate makes us horrible people; it makes us as bad as them, and we are not them. Revenge is never ending. Let's focus on what's good. How are you?"

She shifted her tone. *How can he feel that way after what he's been through?* "Okay, I'll do whatever you want. I'm okay, and I love you. Are you okay?"

"Well I'm talking to you, aren't I? I'm giving you advice, right? I must be pretty healthy to be able to do that," he said in a laugh, his sense of humor rising to the top as it always did. "Now go get your work done, chiquita. You don't want to get fired. That's all we need...more money problems."

"Okay, thanks Papa. I will call you tomorrow. I'm so glad you're okay," she said.

"Me too. Me too," he responded with finesse.

She hung up and pictured him smiling. It set her mind out on the sea, peacefully floating on the water. Things were getting better, little by little.

She walked up to Esmeralda with a puffy red face. "My dad is back."

"What? You haven't seen him since you were little."

"No, not that one. Xavier, my stepdad; he's the one who matters. He turned up in Guadalajara after being detained by ICE for months. They wouldn't let him call anyone and he was in solitary confinement. Such idiots. I'm so glad he's okay, but I'm pissed he had to go through that. It's just wrong."

"Woah, that's crazy," Esmeralda responded. "Something like that happened to my tia. She came out fucked up too. Not sure what happened to her there."

"Makes sense. They treat people like animals. Where do they get off on that? Anyways, I'm so glad he's safe. We didn't know where he was or what had happened to him. My mom was convinced he'd left us, but we knew he hadn't. He's not like that."

Marcus heard them and looked over, his expression softening. "I'm so happy for you," he interjected. "Most of us don't get to see our family again—not after the government takes them." He gave her an uncharacteristic hug. "So is he okay?" he asked.

"I think so. I guess he's been in some prison-like place for the best part of last year. They wouldn't let him make any calls, and we thought he was dead. No one knew where he was."

10:43 p.m.

Lucas barreled down Washington Boulevard, filled with the rage of a man disrespected. No one would talk to him like that, especially not someone like Sergio. *Who the hell does he think he is?* An angst he hadn't felt for months crept up inside of him like an upward winding snake. It was strangling him.

As he boiled about Sergio, his little brother Tyler's face, round and innocent–even in adulthood, suddenly came into view and deepened his discomfort. Just before Tyler had left, moved away from all of them forever, he had said the same thing to Lucas. *You are a horrible person.* The thought hung over him and crushed his skull. Was it true?

He hadn't reacted in violence when his brother said this. Instead he felt nothing and did nothing, but they say apathy is more dangerous than hatred. He felt as if something had fallen off inside of him, as if part of his boyhood innocence had dissolved. Slowly though, over the months that followed Tyler's exodus, apathy melted and anger surfaced. He tried to push it down. It built in him until it bled out. For years, a rush of hate made an entrance every time someone criticized him.

Whenever a dark word was spoken, he would burst into flames and react impulsively, just as he had with Sergio. He felt as if he had very little control over his body in these moments. Sometimes he wondered if that was how The General had felt when he attacked his mother.

With a burst of poison he ran through a red light. *Was he becoming his father?* The world was crashing down on him, his sense of wellbeing flattened.

I'm not a bad person, he thought. His stomach rumbled. *I've got my life together. I'm just like everyone else.*

A billboard up ahead advertised erectile dysfunction and it made him feel even worse: weaker. It seemed that all of the men around him had been falling: Joseph, Sergio, even The General had lost his muster. And then there was Tyler: his face floated in front of him again. Soon Sergio's face overlapped his brother's and replaced it. *What is happening?* He thought. The faces hovered, almost overlapping, and soon became one.

He hated effeminate guys, and it seemed they were becoming more and more common. Women were knocking them down, molding them into clay. The worst part was they seemed to like it.

Last time he'd talked to Tyler he'd seemed so happy with his mundane life, and even Joseph, his formerly hellish brother, was loosening up and accommodating his girlfriend. It was almost as if she ran things. *Disgusting*, he thought. And Sergio, *what an idiot.* He was ridiculous, letting his wife boss him around like that. He would never do that. *We need to get back to how it used to be, when a man was a man*, he thought as he sped around another corner and listened to his heart thump.

He turned the music up–Van Halen was on and it made him feel better. Girls. Girls. Girls.

A recent podcast he'd listened to popped into his mind.

The interview was bloodcurdling–two men talking about how they had regained their strength after enduring years of emasculation. They said exactly what he had been thinking. *We need to get back to the alpha state. They also mentioned that the men who give in and become what their women want them to be, are like children and need to be taught how to thrive again. They had lost their way.*

They were right. He was glad he'd head-butted Sergio. Maybe it would toughen him up a bit. Maybe it was what he needed. In pride, and with a sense of clarity, he began to feel better about himself and accelerated into the dark underpass. His headlights lit everything up and he could see that it was full of tents of all sizes. There was a mix of people lying on the ground in old sleeping bags and a smattering of graffiti on signs and banners. It disgusted him. *Get a fucking job.*

He saw an old woman walking in front of him, sauntering aimlessly down the street, with a long black shawl streaming behind her. She looked gross, like she belonged inside, out of plain sight. He rolled down his window.

"Get off the street old bag," he yelled and spat at her. It felt good and made him laugh to himself. He quickly rolled the window up and glanced back at her through his rearview mirror. He was expecting she'd be scared but instead she smiled a toothless grin and looked as if she was floating above the ground. *Is she a ghost?* He considered, and for a moment the prospect frightened him. She turned her head and he could see her mouth was deformed and resembled a beak. He thought he might be imagining things, but then he noticed a long black feather peaking out beneath her arm.

"What the fuck?" he muttered under his breath as he continued to look back at her. He sped into the night to escape her monstrous form.

What was that? He thought.

As he moved down the street, he saw another unhoused person. She sat on the curb with a huge poppy flower blanket draped around her shoulders. This time he didn't yell because he was unexpectedly overwhelmed with sadness. His mother's image floated into his mind. She had sought out flowers wherever she went and tried to cover herself, and their house, in them whenever she could afford to. Poppies. Morning glory. Chamomile. You name it, she loved it. Suddenly he wanted nothing more than to see her. He looked at his own eyes in the rearview mirror. They were hers–green and bloodshot. He thought back to the beatings, his apathy, even interest, and was disgusted with himself. Maybe he was a bad person.

Where is she? he thought, as he focused on the road again. He hoped she wasn't alone, or even worse, homeless like the bird woman. She'd never had a job, so the chances of her being on the streets were high. He couldn't imagine she had found a way to make it.

What did it mean to make it? He considered this as he drove. He was still at home, as an adult, stuck with The General and Joseph. *Had he made it?* His breath grew shallow and his skin felt tight as it hugged his bones. He pumped the accelerator and skidded around a corner, almost hitting an unhoused man who was pushing a stroller full of cans and assorted finds.

Ahead he saw the bold lights of Hustler's Hub and it felt like a cold drink.

I need an escape, he thought. *That's the problem. Long day. No rest. I deserve this.*

He pulled in and parked the truck. This would solve it.

It wasn't busy and that was fine with him. Maybe he'd get more attention than usual. The club was dimly lit and smelled like a high school gym locker room, but he didn't care. A few men sat in groups while others lingered by the dance floor alone. It was a man's world, the way it should be.

"Can I get a Bud Light?" he asked as he walked up to the bar and signaled the bartender.

"You got it, man," the bartender answered as he glanced over at him, his long black hair tied in a knot behind his neck. He noticed a thin line tattoo on his arm, with the words *lost love.* Lucas thought it cheesy but wanted someone to talk to, so he engaged.

"Slow night, huh?" Lucas said. "Thanks for getting a guy a drink. Man, I need it." He wanted to feel like a good person as Sergio's words kept echoing in his mind. He wasn't a bad person. Hopefully some conversation could make him feel better.

Ignoring Lucas, the bartender set his drink down on a thin white napkin and returned to the back wall to dry out some glasses. Lucas assumed he didn't hear him and gave up. He turned around to scope out the place. He hadn't been to a strip club in a long time, and it felt good, like he was a king. *This is how we used to feel,* he thought. *This is how it should be. Women used to know how to treat a man.* He sipped his light beer slowly and already felt better.

There were two women dancing on a raised stage across the bar: one black woman with long braids, large exposed breasts, and a tiny red thong and a Latina woman with curly dark hair and the curves of a tempest. She wore thin white lace panties, which he preferred. He settled in beneath her and began to feel much better. He was going to get what he deserved.

As he watched the women dance, his mind returned to earlier that evening and the woman at McDonalds. He remembered how good she'd felt when he had her years before. Her young face floated into view and the blood pulsed through him with new energy. She'd seemed scared, powerless even, and that felt good to him. He was in charge there. No one would decide what he could do or take. He would be the master of his domain. He remembered how her cries fell on deaf ears. It was all part of it. He was a man and it was his world, and he aimed to take it back.

11:10 p.m.

Leona gathered her bags and said goodbye to Esmeralda before she walked out. She was overjoyed. Xavier was alive. She wondered if he would be angry that her mom hadn't worked harder to find him, and she also wanted to know if he'd ever be able to get back into their life now that he was stuck in Mexico.

She loved Xavier dearly; she and Jas needed him around. Maybe her mom's depression would subside now that Xavier was back in their lives. Even if they didn't get to see him, it was good to know he was okay, alive.

The strength that had been rising up in her all day came to a peak and it burned in a fiery blaze in her belly. She looked down at the swallow key, still surprised that it too was back in her possession. It was hers, and she would keep it by her side forever. She thought about what Bruja had said–she had been strong when it was missing–and wondered where the power lay: *was it in her or the heirloom?* The glimmer of the golden swallow shone in the street light, and she looked carefully at it–it seemed to be flying off the key, before placing it in her pocket. It would be safe there.

Maybe Bruja was right, she thought. *Maybe the power is inside me.* There was always a possibility but she wouldn't take a chance. She would keep it near just in case. Either way she loved it. It held generations of strength and magic. Nothing can replace that.

As she made her way down 7th Street, the warm night air carried her, and she could see the bus stop sitting way up ahead in the darkness. For a moment, it made her nervous and she had the split second thought of running back to work, but she pushed back the irrational fear. Things were looking up all around her and the day would end well. That's what Bruja had said anyway.

A station wagon drove by with what looked to be a happy family in it.

She wanted that–a normal life—the kind that other people took for granted. The poor dreamed of what the rich saw as boring. The disheveled dreamed of what the secure found commonplace. Only some people could be full of the spirit of adventure and sit and enjoy the beauty of nature. Only some could vacation on islands or take long road trips up the coast with their whole family intact. Only some could plant trees and escape to their beautiful orange blossom-filled backyards. She thought of all of this as she walked past a tent and urine-stained electrical box. The stench was overwhelming. She thought about how cities often carried this smell. It was dirty gutter water, urine, and hot asphalt, but it felt like home to her, but she always wondered if that was healthy. *Is "dirty" really the smell of home?*

Her bags hit her hips as she moved briskly toward the bus stop. A car slowed to a stroll as it passed her and a dark haired man stared for a little too long. There were other people scattered throughout the street, but it was mostly empty. The earlier buses were fine, but the later ones carried people who would ride all night—not the workers on their way home from their minimum wage jobs, but instead who had nowhere to go. She tried to avoid them, but many times she had no choice.

She hopped on and found a seat. She texted Carlos so that he'd be aware of where she was in case she never made it.

I'm on my way. You'll never believe this—Xavier is alive and he's in Mexico with his family. Oh, and I got Atzi's key back! I have so much to tell you.

He'd probably just gotten off of work as well; she assumed he was in transit and knew nothing about Xavier. Suddenly, her mind returned to their earlier conversation about UCLA and she realized she hadn't checked in hours. Her stomach sank as she clicked on the email icon.

Rape Kit

I don't want to be brave; I want to be free.

* * *

Hundreds of thousands of rape kits go untested and sitting in cue in crime storage facilities all over the country. Although the rape victim already came forward, relayed the story of the assault, went through the emotionally taxing experience of submitting evidence of the crime against her body, many of the kits sit untested. Sometimes it's not necessary to analyze the kit because the victim knows who the attacker was, but many times they do not, and are left waiting for their kit to be reviewed. This occurs because many detectives or prosecutors don't request DNA analysis, or if they do, the test kits sit in queue in crime labs. Some people have had to wait years for the results of their rape kit and therefore justice is delayed for them.

To submit a rape kit, the victim has to undergo an invasive full body search for DNA from the assailant, endure a swab of the vagina and/or other body parts that may have been affected, and take a photograph. The entire process takes anywhere from four to six hours. Despite this arduous process, many of the kits are never analyzed.

There are no clear and consistent laws about how to proceed with rape kits and therefore it is left up to the local jurisdiction to decide to do so. This exemplifies the lackluster attitudes that many have regarding rape; women's safety is not a priority.

11:25 p.m.

There was a message:

"Leona Oro-Wolfe, Congratulations! You are UCLA-bound."

She screamed, "Yes!" Some of the riders stared at her in annoyance. "I got in. I got in! I can't believe it!"

She was astounded by the news. It was too good to be real. Her heart jumped vibrantly.

This would change everything, she thought. She'd no longer be in the shadows—no longer deep underwater, barely able to take a breath. This would be her way out—her way to get a car and a real job. This would be her ticket to law school. She hadn't really thought it could be done, but she did it. Most people in her shoes didn't have this type of success, and she knew it. It was just a dream they reached for but were rarely able to grasp, running the marathon without the win–that was how most people lived their lives.

One woman with a head scarf applauded, catching onto the fact that something good had happened.

Leona nodded at her and said, "Thank you."

She dialed Carlos but it went to voicemail. She texted instead.

Call me! It's important.

Her fingers felt for the swallow key and sent a thank you to her ancestors. "I did it," she mumbled as she held the swallow's body in her hand. "I can't believe it, Xochitl! You would be so proud. I know you would."

It seemed as if everything was falling right into its perfect space. All of the terror that had come upon her, all of her tears and late nights, every cycle she wanted to break, it looked as if she was doing it. She'd be the first in our family to go to college and maybe the last to be impoverished. I found myself beaming with pride, and I wanted nothing more than to tell everyone. I screamed at the top of my lungs and my voice echoed in the leaves of the trees. *My granddaughter has risen! She will make something of herself. She will make something of all of us!*

A rush of warmth flowed through Leona's body for the second time that night as she saw a better life unfold before her.

No more peeling lead paint on the windowsills.

No more loud crashes at midnight from the back alley.

No more 99 cent meals at fast food places because they couldn't afford anything healthier.

No more gritting her teeth as she walked home at midnight.

No more being treated like the scum of the earth.

She would be free, and their kids would be free too. It would take continued devotion and a lot of sweat and tears, but she would do it.

This was her opening, and she was going to jump in. The

door was cracked, and she could see the light coming through from the other side. She'd get there and take others with her.

* * *

In the rush of excitement, she quickly grabbed her stuff and jumped off the bus. Her rapid pulse thumped to the beat of opportunity, but I sensed a wicked scent floating through the air.

I cried out to warn her, but she didn't hear me. She was too wrapped up in elation to notice. Xavier was alive and she had gotten into her dream school. What could be better? Carlos would be overjoyed for her; they would celebrate as soon as she got home.

Brimming with happiness, she hustled down the last alley before she'd get to her street. She thought about how long it had taken to get to this point—five long years, during which she almost dropped out multiple times. And she thought of her inner struggle and the demons that continued to gag her. Nothing was going to get her now. This was a metamorphosis! She thought of me and I could see her smile as she remembered how I had once told her that in order for a swallow to learn to fly, it had to practice for two long hours on the ground without giving up. Once it was airborne, the parent flew alongside it to make sure it knew what it was doing.

She was up there now and no longer needed a guide.

* * *

A heavy hand landed on her shoulder, gripping her collar bone as it pulled her back into yesterday.

As the force intensified, she turned to look her offender in the eye and everything, all at once, made sense. It was the man she had seen earlier at work and in this setting she realized that she *did* know him. His white blond curls stuck to his sweaty red forehead and the drooping bags under his eyes made him look like he'd been awake for days.

"Now you remember," he said as he held her there. "I knew it would come to you."

Her eyes widened and she gasped as he tightened his grip on her shoulder, pulling her neck inward towards him. "Fuck...," she yelled as she panicked, losing her balance and newfound strength as the world began to spin and she remembered the day everything first fell apart. "Let go. I'm not yours to..." she muttered helplessly. It felt as if her body was separating from her mind and she vowed to stay present. *I have to keep hold of myself. I have to be here,* she thought as he moved in closer. The image of yellow doors rushed back to her. Red rugs hanging. The pain in her body. The tinny smell of fear. All of it was as clear as day as she stood there in the vast emptiness looking terror in the eye.

He moved towards her and shoved her violently, slamming her head against the concrete wall of the backside of a liquor store and moving his hand up to her neck. "Shut the fuck up. You're what I want you to be," he mumbled in aggression as he reached down with one hand to undo his pants. Her belly burned with anger and fire.

This can't be happening. Not again.

"Basta!" she yelled and shoved his elbow aside, trying to knock his hand away. Though she was scared to death, she imagined she could escape if she used her wit. As the pressure on her neck tightened, she was able to wriggle like a snake and get loose. Once he lost his grip, he became angrier. She ducked under his arm and backed into the street to find the light and try to get out, but her vision blurred and her dizziness returned.

Yellow doors. Red rugs. A face pushed onto the leather couch. Her world spun more as she tried to steady herself.

I've got to stay present. Breathe. Breathe. He cannot win this time, she told herself.

Adrenaline pumped into her body. He reached for her again like she was a lamb and took a hold of her body.

"This will be fun," he grunted and tried to pull her in. "You didn't mind it..."

"No," she spit into his face. "I'm not going down..." She struggled to move away from him, kicking his shin and trying to aim for his groin, but was unable to reach him.

"Help! Fire!" Leona screamed as she had learned to do many years before. Someone had told her that if you yell fire, people will pay attention because they think it might affect them, and call for help.

He leaned in, regaining his grasp on her neck. "You know you want this. You wanted it back then, and you want it now."

"Get the fuck away from me," she yelled and tried to kick him again with her heavy black boot. He kept his hold on her this time. She felt herself begin to freeze—like she as a teen—but worked to summon all of her strength and melt the ice of the person she used to be.

When he shifted his grip to her neck and pushed her hard against the wall, the fuel of indignation raged within her. She gasped for air as she fought, punching and dodging the best she could. Suddenly, Atzi's face appeared, just as it had earlier that morning in her nightmare and she remembered the key. Her fingers found it with her free hand and it flew out like a bird escaping a cage. She grasped the swallow and held the key between her fingers, blade out.

Yellow doors. Loud screams. Footsteps. Pulsating blood. Hunger. Starvation. Yearning. The cold and the hot. The fiery will. The ache of mothers. The ache of the ages. The climb into the light. The breaking of the cycle. The beating of a young heart. Rebirth. We won't take this any more. This was for her aunt. This was for herself.

Enough.

With a fierce yell and guttural angst, she shoved the golden key into his right eye with all of her might, viciously cutting him open and watching as he stammered. The edge dug into him and stabbed the palm of her hand simultaneously, making the shape of a bird. He fell to the ground in shock, oozing blood in huge gobs. There was more blood than she had imagined to be possible from such a small puncture, but she was glad. He deserved to feel the blow; it was as if he was bleeding for everyone he'd attacked.

"What the hell!" he yelped and held his eye, trying to stop the bleeding and get to his feet. His eye was swelling quickly and he seemed to be getting worried.

"Basta, Fucker!" she spit furiously at him as she backed away. "You're pathetic."

In this moment she felt herself ascending and imagined all of the women rising with her. A flock of starlings flitted above her as if shocked by the yelling. Before he could get back to his feet, she pivoted and flew away quickly into the light of the full moon, leaving the darkness behind her as the vision of men on horses shattered on the pavement.

Roxana Ruiz

I don't want to be brave; I want to be free.

* * *

Roxana Ruiz was beaten and raped by a man she'd had hung out with earlier that night in her hometown of Oaxaca. After finishing up her work making french fries at a food stand, she hung out with the man she had just gotten to know and allowed him to stay the night on a mattress on her floor near her bed because he said he was far from home.

In the middle of the night, however, he got onto her bed, tore off her clothes, beat her, and then assaulted her. She tried to defend herself while he was hitting her and she broke his nose. He threatened to take her life and she fought back. While defending herself, she killed him. After this, she was afraid so she put his body in a bag and dragged it outside. The police happened to see her. She expressed that he had raped her and that she murdered him in self defense but the police never did a forensic inspection. As a result she was prosecuted.

She has been given a sentence of six years in prison, but she maintains that she would have been dead if she didn't kill him. According to Ruiz, "It's evident that the state wants to shut us up, wants us to be submissive, wants us closed up inside, wants us dead." This type of sentence in sexual assault cases regarding the victim is not uncommon in countries all over the world as proper procedures to identify rape are overlooked and the common thinking is that women are to blame for the assault.

11:58 p.m.

When Leona reached home, she was out of breath, and the front door was unlocked. She burst in and looked directly at Carlos.

He peered at her, questioning. "What happened? Are you okay?" He asked as he moved in closer and took her in his arms, sensing something was wrong. His back was still damp from the shower he'd just gotten out.

She pulled back and looked at him as tears began to stream down her face. "Yes, I'm okay. Actually, I'm well..." she said, breathing heavily. Her heart was still racing from the fight. "I made it. I'm finally what I need to be."

He gasped, "What do you mean?"

"I mean exactly what I said. I made it," she answered as power and self-realization jolted through her body. "It's all going to be okay. No one is going to hold me down."

"Good..." he said, not understanding (because how could he?) and pulled her in towards him, happy to see her empowered state.

As she let herself slip into his embrace she saw my picture

and Cecilia's on the bookshelf behind her, realizing she hadn't been alone.

I glowed back at her. Energy never dies; it lives on in the people and the air around you, influencing everything by lending a hand and planting a kiss. It exists in the ether and anything we want it to.

Leona bowed her head slightly in the direction of our faces and smiled.

Nothing has ever made me feel so good as this very moment. My Leona, the beautiful young bird I watched grow up and navigate the tricky violent path of life, was free. She was brave too, although she didn't want to be. She shouldn't need to be, but until men stop raping, we will always need to be brave.

"What's changed?" Carlos asked. "You're different."

"I'm just done accepting things," she said. "I'm done hiding."

"What do you mean 'hiding'?" he continued as he stepped back to look her over. He wanted to understand everything. She was dripping with sweat and looked as if she'd been in a fight.

"I'm done hiding in fear. I'm going to build my life and bring others up with me. I won."

"Great, but how?" he asked.

"I'll do everything I want and do it with confidence. I'll fight back. We all will. We're not going to take it anymore."

"This is what I've been waiting for, Ona. You've had it in you all along. I knew it. You have always been strong," he said.

"No, I haven't. You said that, but I wasn't. Now I realize

what's necessary though. It shouldn't be, but it is," she said. "I had to fight back and see that I could make it. I had to go through this churning and burning—this bursting out of my skin—to see that I could survive. We're too nice. We need to stop it. We need to stand tall."

He suddenly noticed a speck of blood on her brow and touched it with his finger. "Wait, what's this? Did something *actually* happen?" he asked. "Did someone touch you?"

She could see anger beginning to form on his face and his bare chest beginning to tighten. She loved him and appreciated his desire to protect her, but she didn't want it. The issue was that she shouldn't need to be protected because men shouldn't rape. The issue was rape.

"Yes, everything happened," she said as she pulled him in, and moved his hand away from her head, kissing him feverishly. "I love you. We're going to be okay. Everything is going to be okay."

He looked at her with wide eyes, surprised by the woman who stood in front of him. She had a new fire in her belly and seemed to have transformed into a goddess of strength over the course of one day.

She stood strong, in her tiny form, as they kissed, and with this, Leona let Atzi's key fly to the ground along with all that sought to devour her.

Statistics on Rape

* * *

According to the Rape & Abuse, Incest National Network (RAINN)

433,648 people are raped in the US every year.
90% of victims are women (1 out of 6 women)
63,000 of victims are children (ages 12-17)
Most assaults happen at home (about 55%)

Need Help?
For an emergency, call 911

For trauma recovery or prevention:
RAINN
rainn.org
800-656-HOPE

National Sexual Violence Resource Center
nsvrc.org

Never ever give up

Women

You don't owe men a fucking thing.
Cherish the ones who respect you.
Empower your sisters.
Be loud, be bold. Be full.

Mothers and Fathers

Raise your sons and daughters the same.
Do not perpetuate gender stereotypes.
Empower them to be empathetic.
Model feminism.

Notes on "I don't want to be brave; I want to be free" Excerpts

Dumpster

Stack, L. (2016, June 8). *In Stanford Rape Case, Brock Turner Blamed Drinking and Promiscuity*. The New York Times. https://www.nytimes.com/2016/06/09/us/brock-turner-blamed-drinking-and-promiscuity-in-sexual-assault-at-stanford.html

Times, N. Y. (2019, September 5). Court statement of Stanford rape victim. *The New York Times*. https://www.nytimes.com/interactive/2016/06/08/us/stanford-rape-victim-statement.html

The Fearless One

BBC News. (2020, March 20). Nirbhaya case: Four Indian men executed for 2012 Delhi bus rape and murder. *BBC News*. https://www.bbc.com/news/world-asia-india-51969961

Las Hijas de Violencia

AJ+. (2016, January 27). *Fighting street harassers with confetti guns and punk rock* [Video]. YouTube. https://www.youtube.com/watch?v=0ze4AH_5kJw

Gaga

Savage, B. M. (2021, May 21). Lady Gaga had a "psychotic break" after sexual assault left her pregnant. *BBC News*. https://www.bbc.com/news/entertainment-arts-57199018

The Rapist is You

Colectivo Registro Callejero. (2019, November 26). *Performance colectivo Las Tesis*

"Un violador en tu camino" [Video]. YouTube. https://www.youtube.com/watch?v=aB7r6hdo3W4

Demented Doctor

Read Rachael Denhollander's full victim impact statement about Larry Nassar. (2018, January 30). CNN. https://www.cnn.com/2018/01/24/us/rachael-denhollander-full-statement/index.html

Biles: I blame an entire system that enabled, perpetrated Nassar's abuse. (2021b, September 16). [Video]. NBC News. https://www.nbcnews.com/politics/congress/we-have-been-failed-simone-biles-breaks-down-tears-recounting-n1279255

New lawsuit alleges Larry Nassar drugged, raped and impregnated teen at MSU. (2018, September 12). NBC News. https://www.nbcnews.com/news/us-news/new-lawsuit-alleges-larry-nassar-drugged-raped-impregnated-teen-michigan-n908681

Asian Fetish

Gupta, A. H. (2021, March 19). Tales of Racism and Sexism, from 3 leading Asian-American women. *The New York Times.* https://www.nytimes.com/2021/03/19/us/racism-sexism-asian-american-women.html

Morality Police

Pelham, B. L. (2024, March 8). *Mahsa Amini: Iran responsible for "physical violence" leading to death, UN says.* https://www.bbc.com/news/world-middle-east-68511112

Tarana Burke

Mosley, T. (2021, September 29). "Me Too" founder Tarana Burke says Black girls' trauma shouldn't be ignored. *NPR.* https: //www.npr.org/2021/09/29/1041362145/me-too-founder-tarana-burke-says-black-girls-trauma-shouldnt-be-ignored

Off to College

David Cantor, Bonnie Fisher, Susan Chibnall, Reanna Townsend, et. al. Association of American Universities (AAU), Report on the AAU Campus Climate Survey on Sexual Assault and Sexual Misconduct (January 17, 2020).

Rape Kit

Joyful Heart Foundation. (2023). *Why the Backlog Exists.* End The Backlog. Retrieved December 10, 2023, from https://www.endthebacklog.org/what-is-the-backlog/why-the-backlog-exists/

Roxana Ruiz

Roxana Ruiz, woman who killed rapist, sentenced to 6 years in Mexican prison. (2023,

May 17). CBS News. https://www.cbsnews.com/news/roxana-ruiz-killed-rapist-sentenced-6-years-prison-mexico/

Stats on Rape

Scope of the problem: Statistics | RAINN. (n.d.). https://www.rainn.org/statistics/scope-problem

About the Author

Lucia Maz writes poetry, short stories, editorials, and novels. Basta is her debut novel. She is also the author of a short story and poetry collection, A Tiny Existence, which debuted in August 2025.

In addition to writing, Maz is the head of La Luce Literary, a creative smorgasbord that consists of writing consulting, indie publishing, and gatherings for artists.

Maz is a proud first-generation college student and feminist. She is a lover of nature, an eternal optimist, and a purveyor of 90s hip hop, art deco architecture, civil rights movements, philosophy, and art in every form. She lives near the ocean in Southern California with her partner and their beautiful children.

Luciamaz.com

www.ingramcontent.com/pod-product-compliance
Lightning Source LLC
LaVergne TN
LVHW100519110826
845146LV00002B/698

* 9 7 9 8 9 9 9 5 9 9 1 1 7 *